P9-BZM-360

"I'm going home tomorrow, Blake."

In an instant his hands tightened on her yielding body. "It's too late. If you had really wanted to escape, you should have gone that first day." There was a strained silence before he added grimly. "Except that I think I would have followed you."

"I know."

Finley closed her eyes and listened to the thunder of his heart against her cheek. She knew what was going to happen. Dreamily she thought that her life had been a preparation for this, and the blood sang exultantly through her veins.

He said something, a statement of need so blatant that her eyes flew open and she thought in sudden useless panic, *What am I getting myself into*? They both knew it couldn't work!

"Too late—" he said, and his mouth came down to hers.

ROBYN DONALD, her husband and their two children make their home in the far north of New Zealand, where they indulge their love for outdoor life in general and sailing in particular. She keeps a file of clippings, photographs and a diary that she confides, "is useful in my work as well as for settling family arguments!"

Books by Robyn Donald

HARLEQUIN PRESENTS

623—THE GUARDED HEART
631—RETURN TO YESTERDAY
649—AN OLD PASSION
665—THE GATES OF RANGITATAU
696—A DURABLE FIRE
904—AN UNBREAKABLE BOND
936—LONG JOURNEY BACK
952—CAPTIVES OF THE PAST
976—A WILLING SURRENDER

HARLEQUIN ROMANCE

2391—BAY OF STARS
2437—ICEBERG

Don't miss any of our special offers. Write to us at the following address for information on our newest releases.

Harlequin Reader Service
901 Fuhrmann Blvd., P.O. Box 1397, Buffalo, NY 14240
Canadian address: P.O. Box 603,
Fort Erie, Ont. L2A 5X3

ROBYN DONALD

country of the heart

Harlequin Books

TORONTO • NEW YORK • LONDON
AMSTERDAM • PARIS • SYDNEY • HAMBURG
STOCKHOLM • ATHENS • TOKYO • MILAN

To Rebecca, and Sally, and Haydn,
who provided the island,
and their dog Spey,
who is Blackie.

Harlequin Presents first edition January 1988
ISBN 0-373-11040-5

Original hardcover edition published in 1987
by Mills & Boon Limited

Copyright © 1987 by Robyn Donald. All rights reserved.
Philippine copyright 1987. Australian copyright 1987.
Except for use in any review, the reproduction or utilization of
this work in whole or in part in any form by any electronic,
mechanical or other means, now known or hereafter invented,
including xerography, photocopying and recording, or in any
information storage or retrieval system, is forbidden without
the permission of the publisher, Harlequin Enterprises Limited,
225 Duncan Mill Road, Don Mills, Ontario, Canada M3B 3K9.

All the characters in this book have no existence outside the
imagination of the author and have no relation whatsoever to
anyone bearing the same name or names. They are not even
distantly inspired by any individual known or unknown to the
author, and all incidents are pure invention.

The Harlequin trademarks, consisting of the words
HARLEQUIN PRESENTS and the portrayal of a Harlequin,
are trademarks of Harlequin Enterprises Limited and are
registered in the Canada Trade Marks Office; the portrayal
of a Harlequin is registered in the United States Patent
and Trademarks Office.

Printed in U.S.A.

CHAPTER ONE

HIGH summer!

The very words had a magic all their own. Finley MacMillan pushed hair the colour of dark chocolate away from her small face and rolled over on to her back, stretching her slight body luxuriously across the rug. Long lashes flicked drowsily as she gazed up into the silver and green canopy of the pohutukawa tree. A wide yawn revealed small teeth before fading into a sleepy, satisfied smile as her lids closed over eyes as green as the leaves above her.

Just before sleep claimed her, she decided there was something to be gained after all from pneumonia and its debilitating aftermath. In her case the 'something' was three weeks on Motuaroha. An intriguing name; what had caused the Maoris who once had lived here to christen their home the 'island of love'? Resolving to find out the reason, she yawned once more. The love could go hang, she didn't have time for it. She was more than content to lie in the shade and listen to the silken whisper of the waves on the beach below, the faint putter of an outboard in the gulf and the muted shouts of a couple of tireless tennis addicts as they exhausted themselves on the hotel courts.

High noon in summer was siesta time. A smug little smile curled Finley's mouth as she let sleep reclaim her.

She woke to war. For a moment, sick panic held her huddled in a small bundle as her mind strove to make sense of the vicious growls and snarls which rendered the air hideous. The tumult was far too close for comfort and sounded, at the very least, as though a pack of wolves were quarrelling over whose right it was to kill the unfortunate human in their sights.

When it became obvious that she was still intact, she opened her eyes. What she saw jerked her bolt upright, yelling, 'No! No you don't. No!'

Both dogs, the emaciated black spaniel and the sleek belligerent cattle dog, recognising the authentic voice of authority, broke off the argument, each head whipping to face her with identical expressions of chagrin and irritation.

'Sit!' she shouted as reinforcement. To her surprise both rumps hit the ground. But the cattle dog, well fed and impudent, ignored the remains of her lunch which lay strewn on the ground, while the spaniel's eyes were fixed on the nearest scrap of food as it drooled in a way that smote Finley's heart.

'Oh, you poor starved thing,' she said, noting the way the skin was stretched tightly over protruding ribs. The tangled matted coat was dull and dirty, the dark eyes glazed with a hunger too insistent for the spaniel to fear her or the much bigger cattle dog.

Ignoring the fact that during her sleep her bikini top had slipped to her waist, Finley reached for a large roll, removed the plastic wrapping and proffered it.

The cattle dog whined, its tail thumping the ground as the smaller dog swallowed with a slavering speed which revealed how close to starving it was.

'I wonder if I should give you any more,' Finley said thoughtfully. 'If you were human that roll would have been too much, but dogs are tougher than your average *Homo sapiens*. Still, any more might make you sick.'

A piteous whine seemed to indicate a definite negative. Superimposed over it was the sound of a horse's hooves. Finley's head swerved sideways. A few yards away, marking the boundary between the hotel grounds and the cattle and sheep station which occupied the greater part of the island, was a wire fence. On the other side, a horse was cantering towards them; judging by the expression on the tanned face of its rider he was appreciating to the full his view of Finley's small, high breasts and slender legs.

'Oh, hell,' she muttered as she dragged up the wayward top, despising the lack of self-confidence which roused the heat now suffusing all her visible skin. She must be, she decided bitterly, the only woman in the world whose legs blushed.

After all, nowadays lots of women went topless at the beach. Even in New Zealand! This farm-hand wasn't to know how embarrassed she was by her temporary nakedness.

She braced herself for a comment or a knowing smile, but his first words were for his dog.

'Here, Blue!'

The cattle dog got to its feet, grinned at Finley and trotted casually back through the fence and up to the horse. There, a respectful distance from the hooves, it sat down to enjoy a good scratch.

Unaware that she was smiling, Finley looked up—and up—and up. The horse was huge, a roan with a gentle, enquiring face, and the man on it was huge, too. Well, not huge, exactly. Not lumbering, or clumsy, or giant-like. But big. Finley quite frequently bemoaned her miniature dimensions but never more so than now. With a wary, fascinated gaze, she watched as the intruder swung down and looped the reins over the nearest post. He tipped his hat to her, revealing hair the colour of ripe wheat.

'That dog,' he said pleasantly, 'is a stray.'

'I can see that. He's also starving.'

The amber eyes which were searching her face so diligently gleamed with amusement. 'I'm not responsible for that.'

'I didn't suppose you were.' Another stupid blush heated her skin. Lord, but he made her feel a fool! She began again with somewhat exaggerated patience, 'What do you think I should do with him?'

He glanced indifferently down at the dog then caught her eyes once more in the glowing fire of his. 'He's not wearing a collar, so presumably his previous owners don't want him back. Too soft-hearted to have him killed instantly, I suppose, so they've dumped him from a boat. He should be shot.'

Finley discovered that she would not like to make an enemy of this man. The deep incisive voice could express biting contempt, and when he had spoken of the dog's owners his strong features had hardened in a way which sent an odd little *frisson* up her spine.

Then the harsh expression relaxed into a smile of such blazing charm that she had to swallow before she could protest. 'But you can't shoot him! It's not his fault he's here. Poor little fellow, look at him, he's absolutely terrified.'

She bent down to run her fingers through the tousled curls on top of the lifted head, ignoring the stranger's command to desist. Instantly, her hand was wrenched away and held in a calloused grip which came close to hurting. Finley lifted furious eyes, hiding the shock his touch gave her with an imperious face. Before she could say anything, the stranger released her and in an oddly blank voice said, 'Never touch a stray dog. Some have no inhibitions about biting the hand that strokes them.'

Shaken, Finley looked down at the dog. 'You wouldn't do that, would you?'

The dog responded to the caressing note in her voice with a little shiver of pleasure, his short tail beating enthusiastically on the ground.

'He's almost certainly covered in fleas,' the stranger observed mockingly. 'And ticks.'

'Ugh!'

'In his ears especially.'

Finley promptly knelt and began to inspect the floppy ears with the intent expression of someone who knows what she is doing. She ignored the man until she was confident that there were no ticks or other forms of life hiding in the ears.

'You did that very competently,' he observed, stooping to run a lean brown hand over the pitifully thin body of the animal. It whimpered, but suffered his touch. 'Have you had dogs?'

'No, I'm a doctor.' Finley spoke absently, watching those strong fingers assess the dog with skill and gentleness.

'A doctor?'

She allowed herself a small sigh before looking up to meet his startled eyes. They were not so much amber as gold, a strange lion-colour emphasised by dark brows and lashes. The lashes were incredible, curling on both upper and lower lids like a model's. Finley knew that she was staring, but was quite unable to stop. The face those remarkable eyes illuminated had little of beauty in it, unless it was the uncompromising beauty of strength. He wore his character in his face, and no one seeing him would ever doubt the force and power of that character.

'Yes, a doctor,' she said haughtily, indignant because she had been staring at him like a love-struck adolescent. She tore her glance away and finished, 'My name is Finley MacMillan. Contrary to all appearances, I'm out of school.'

'How far out?'

She said wearily, 'I'm twenty-six.'

Very gravely, he extended a hand. 'How do you do, Dr MacMillan.'

'I'm only a very junior doctor,' she explained just as gravely, as they shook hands over the bemused dog.

'You don't look old enough to be a medical student.' He sounded sympathetic. 'I'm Blake Caird, I live here, and I'm thirty-four years old. I'm not married,' he added pensively, regarding her with eyes which were brilliant with laughter.

Uncomfortable and a little ruffled, Finley retrieved her hand, wishing that his height and size didn't make her feel quite so inadequate. She had to tip her head back to get a good view of his face!

'I don't usually call myself a doctor.' She floundered for a moment before finishing. 'Because I'm so small, people tend to treat me as if I were a child. I need all the dignity I can get!'

'I know the feeling.'

'Oh, but surely——'

'If one is over six feet two and built like a truck, most people assume one has the mentality of your average truck. You didn't happen to mention if there is a husband about?'

She blushed, and laughed at the lurking laughter in his expression. 'No, I haven't had time to acquire one. Is there anything wrong with the dog?'

'No, he's in surprisingly good nick. He was well cared for until he was dumped. He'll soon pick up condition once he's fed properly. What are you going to do with him?'

'Me? I can't . . .' She stared helplessly down as the dog leaned his head against her knee and gazed worshipfully upwards with an intensity which worried her. 'I can't look after him,' she wailed.

'He's fallen in love with you.'

'But I'm staying at the hotel. I can't keep a dog there.'

White teeth gleamed against the dark tan of his face. Pushing his hat back on to his head, he said carelessly, 'Oh, tell Mike Cloud to find him a place. He's a sucker for a pretty face. Stray animals too, probably.'

'Yes, but——' One of the few provisos laid down by the hotel seemed suddenly burned into her brain. 'Dogs aren't allowed on the island. You know that, you're from the farm. Dogs chase sheep and kill lambs and frighten cattle. He might get shot.'

'If he's managed to avoid it so far I'd say he's intelligent enough to keep away from anyone likely to shoot him,' he said drily. 'Keep him on a leash.'

'I haven't got a leash! And even if I did, even if I could keep him here, I couldn't when I get back home. Do you know what sort of hours I work? Slavery isn't the word for it. Dogs are sociable animals, they need company. And I live in a flat. It wouldn't be fair to keep him locked up without company for so long.'

'Then have him put down.'

For the first time since childhood, and to her intense humiliation, Finley stamped her foot. His calm callousness infuriated and repelled her into loss of control. 'Oh, you—you——'

He said nothing, merely watched with the faintest lift of an eyebrow, but that was enough to call into play a never-needed, primeval female instinct. Without volition, she took a step backwards. His size became suddenly intimidating. He must, she thought warily, be at least six feet four and, far from being built like a truck, he was perfectly in proportion, with shoulders wide enough to block out the world. They tapered to a lean waist and hips and strongly muscled legs which went on for eternity. Serviceable working clothes, khaki trousers and a shirt with sleeves rolled up beyond the elbows, served to accentuate the blatant masculinity which assaulted her senses.

He didn't need to be conventionally handsome. What he had was as potent as wizardry, a blending of strength and sensuality which was a lure and a temptation to femininity.

'I *am* a lot bigger than you, but I only become dangerous at full moon,' he said, watching her narrowly.

Finley smiled, trying rather desperately for the easy cameraderie she normally enjoyed with the opposite sex. 'I think you might be about as harmless as the average tiger,' she returned, realising too late how provocative she had managed to sound.

Those incredible lashes only half hid his shrewd scrutiny. 'It's a well-known fact that big men are slow,' he offered, returning her smile with interest.

'Really?' Brows dark as sable climbed her forehead. 'You'll understand if I say that I think you might be the exception, won't you? I'm sorry I flinched, it was stupid of me. I wasn't expecting you to look as my father used to look when I was throwing a tantrum.'

Fortunately, because she was beginning to gabble, the dog caught her attention. He had improved the time by demolishing the rest of her lunch and was now thoughtfully nosing the bag in which the food had been packed.

'No!' she commanded, afraid he might choke on the plastic.

Instantly, he cowered away.

'Oh, you poor old thing,' Finley said remorsefully, 'he's been beaten, you can tell. Never mind ...' and she dropped on her knees to comfort him, crooning in a way which had always been successful with babies and children.

The dog liked it, too. A pink tongue whisked out to touch the point of her chin while the dark eyes were fixed on hers with unadulterated adoration.

'Oh, what am I going to do with you?' she asked beneath her breath.

Blake Caird said mockingly. 'If you won't have it put down and you can't keep it yourself, you will just have to find it a good home.'

'Would you like a dear little spaniel? He's terribly affectionate and——'

Laughter lines creased his face as he reached down an imperative hand and pulled her upright. 'No, I do not want a dog, I have enough of my own. I've never heard that spaniels are noted for being good working dogs, though I have no doubt he'd be willing enough.'

His hand was calloused and hard and warm, and he was in no hurry to let her go. A thread of response shivered the length of her backbone. Uneasily, she tugged and as he released her she stepped away, dredging frantically for a bit of information from a childhood spent in a small farming town. 'But you don't make pets of your working dogs, do you? Wouldn't you like a pet?'

In a grave voice, belied by his laughing eyes, he said, 'I'm afraid not. Like you, I work long hours. However, if you want me to, I'll look after him until you go back home.'

'For almost three weeks?' She looked from him to the expectant dog and back again, seeking help. She got none. When he wanted, those strong features could be irritatingly bland. Unconsciously, her teeth worried her lower lip. At last she said, 'That's very kind of you. Thank you.'

Her smile was impulsive and warm, radiating her small neat features into a swift blaze of beauty. She was as perfect as a figurine, the pale gold silk of her skin broken only by the white bikini.

There was no answering smile from Blake Caird. His half closed eyes glittered as they scanned her face; for a moment his skin was heated by dusky colour and the striking framework of his face sprang into starker prominence.

Swallowing nervously, Finley turned away. She knew what that intent hungry look meant and she was not ready for it, she did not want to be desirable in his eyes.

In a quick involuntary reflex action she picked up the oversized T-shirt she used as a cover-up and pulled it over her head.

'How will you get him to go home with you?' she asked, in a voice slightly more high-pitched than normal.

'He'll come with Blue.' He sounded detached, quite indifferent, and nothing could have been more impersonal than his subsequent farewell and the expression with which he said it.

Finley watched from beneath her lashes as he climbed the fence and swung on to the horse. It was safe now to admire the lithe smoothness of his movements and the combination of strength and skill he used to calm the sudden eruption of high spirits in the roan.

But all of his expertise could not coax the stray to leave Finley.

At last, mildly exasperated, he said, 'Just stay here until I get back,' and set the horse across the hillside with Blue in smug pursuit.

In her turn exasperated by that casual command, Finley collapsed on to the rug and surveyed the stubborn little spaniel with wry amusement. 'You,' she told him, 'are quite unscrupulous. I know that this sudden touching affection is based on the food I gave you. He won't let you starve, you know. Here, you had better have the rest of this water.'

He appreciated the mineral water she had carried in an insulated flask, drinking it noisily before resting his head on her feet and going politely to sleep.

Finley sat with clasped hands over her knees, ostensibly surveying the broad sweep of the gulf before her. In reality, her eyes saw nothing but Blake Caird's rough-hewn features. He was, she decided dreamily, the most exciting man she had ever seen. Those astounding eyes! And a mouth which gave absolutely nothing away. Did those authoritative curves ever relax into tenderness? It was hard to imagine, but she would be willing to bet her amethyst earrings that he was more complex than the physically intriguing exterior revealed.

Idly, to dampen the excitement which ran like quicksilver through her veins, she occupied herself by finding adjectives to describe him. Masterful was definitely on the list, and yes, arrogant in a pleasant way. And sexy. Well, sexy as hell, and aware of his personal magnetism but too intelligent to trade on it. And, although she was certain that he had quite a temper, she decided that 'bad-tempered' did not do him justice. There was too much self-control written in that tough face; she found herself speculating with a delicious little shiver how he would react if that restraint was breached.

It was an old habit of hers, this categorising of people. She had learnt to do it at a time of great stress; somehow her search for the exact descriptive word or phrase distanced those emotions which had the power to disturb her. So she let her mind wander, a little smile pulling at the disciplined line of her mouth as she labelled Blake and dispatched him to an appropriate slot in her memory. Not that it was as simple as it usually was. He possessed a vitality which made it difficult to relegate him to a set of adjectives.

The soporific zithering of cicadas in the tree above produced another attack of weariness. For a while she resisted it but eventually she succumbed, curling into the rug. The dog lay as close as he could without touching her, his eyes fixed on the pure serene contours of her face.

The distant sound of an engine brought the stray's ears up. Finley didn't stir, not even when the man approached. The faint warning rumble from the spaniel was ignored. For long moments Blake looked down at the slight figure sprawled in the innocent adandon of sleep, his expression completely impassive.

It was the repetition of her name which woke Finley.

Yawning, stretching, she curved instinctively into a posture of defence.

It was like looking up the long slopes of a mountain. He stood with his hands on his hips, booted feet slightly apart, and watched her with a cool interest which shredded the cloak of confidence she normally wore. As if guilty of some crime she flung an arm across her face. Only for a moment, however. It was an effort of will to pull her arm away but she did it, sitting up proudly; she stared into that harsh face, resistance chiselling her features into cold maturity.

It seemed like for ever that their eyes duelled, green clashing with amber while the spaniel's warning became a growl. At last, without any acknowledgement of that sudden, stark tension, Blake stooped and extended a hand. It was like a defeat to accept it, yet Finley saw her own small one engulfed and was lifted to her feet in a smooth, effortless movement.

He smiled, a smile of recognition and sympathetic comprehension at the bewilderment she couldn't hide. His skin was deep gold against the pale silk of hers, his fingers long and powerful and possessive around the fine bones of her hand and wrist. And from that firm grip, from those tanned fingers, sensation spread through her body in a wave of heat which seared into every cell like flashfire and left her trembling, her eyes trapped painfully by the narrowed intensity of his.

'I don't——' she said numbly, then broke off into a gasp as he lifted her hand and kissed the inside of her wrist where her pulse beat like a cornered thing in the blue prison of her vein.

'Neither do I,' he drawled, surveying her flushed face with enigmatic enquiry, 'but I'm looking forward to finding out.'

He gave her back her hand and she frowned, grabbing for some tatters of composure. 'I don't know what you mean,' she said repressively, turning away to hide her embarrassment.

He made no answer, but she saw his mouth ease into a smile as he bent to pick up the rug. For such a big man he moved with a lithe ease which reminded her of the smooth precision of a predator. Not exactly graceful, he was too big to be described as that, but with the balance and poise of a man with complete confidence in his body and himself.

Giving herself a mental shake, Finley seized the bag which had held her lunch and went meekly enough towards the Land Rover parked just through the fence.

'I must have been tired,' she said foolishly. 'I didn't hear you coming at all.'

'Have you been ill?'

She shot him a surprised look. 'Yes,' she admitted reluctantly. 'Pneumonia, and then stupidly I went back to work too soon. Which is why I'm lying about in the sun collecting stray dogs and pretending to be a beach bunny.'

'You're too thin,' he objected. 'Beach bunnies are very well endowed, with lots of very white teeth and a nice line in girlish squeals. No beach bunny worth her rabbit's tail would pat a dog in the certain knowledge that he had fleas. Or let him and his fleas go to sleep on her feet.'

He had a wicked smile when he wanted to use it, and his eyes gleamed in sly complicity. Finley laughed, rather grateful that they had reached the fence and she didn't have to reply. Blake held the wires apart for her to climb through and, by the time she had straightened up and coaxed the dog beneath the wire, Blake was over and smiling down at her with the same wry comprehension which had startled her before. It was as though they shared a secret, the import and meaning of which he assumed she understood.

Attraction, she thought loftily, as she was put into the

Land Rover. The spaniel scrabbled up to crouch quivering at her feet. As Blake strode around to the driver's side she eyed him covertly. Yes, that was what it was, the chemistry which a multitude of poets had lauded so feelingly. Desire, they called it, or passion; some unfortunates called it lust. It was happening all the time. He was a gorgeous specimen of a man, with that wheat-blond hair and striking profile and the other physical attributes, like the width of those shoulders and the powerful lines of his body. Naturally he was attractive. Any woman in her right mind would be interested in that raw animal charisma.

And if her mind was above physical things like the play of his thigh muscles beneath the material of his trousers and the masterful jut of his chin, there was the fact that he possessed the kind of authority and self-assurance which was a definite challenge. He was also, Finley supplied hastily, basically kind, or he would have left her and the dog to their fate.

If, however, you were Finley MacMillan, with an exciting and satisfying future planned and within reach, you backed very swiftly away from such challenges. Blake Caird was probably an experienced and skilful lover, but although disarmingly pleasant he was an exceedingly dangerous man, the sort it might be almost impossible to forget.

Still, it couldn't hurt to be sociable. So she responded affably to his laconic, entertaining conversation as they drove over the short green grass, then down a narrow fenced road which followed the bony spine of the island until they began the descent towards an exquisite bay.

'Homestead Bay,' Blake informed her. 'Named for obvious reasons.'

'Oh, it's beautiful.' Finley's gaze moved appreciatively over the complex of stockyards and sheds almost hidden behind great Norfolk Island pines, towards the house

which dominated the bay. She made an odd little noise
deep in her throat, her hand clamping in sudden entreaty
over his on the steering wheel.

Obediently he stopped the vehicle, saying nothing as
she jumped down and ran a few steps so that she could
see more clearly.

It was an astounding sight in this drowsy South Pacific
landscape. She said incredulously, 'I don't believe it!'

'Sir James Reed built it on the profits he made from
the gold mines. As you can see, he'd travelled in Greece.'

'It's out of this world.'

Built on a little plateau above the beach, the Greek
revival house was faced by broad galleries supported by
Ionic pillars of the same pale stone as the rest of the
edifice. It glowed, serene and elegant in acres of garden
above the wide sweep of the beach and the the blue
laughter of the channel between Motuaroha and the
mainland.

'It looks like a cross between the Parthenon and an
ante-bellum mansion,' Finley said softly. 'It should look
incongruous, but somehow it's completely at home here.
Lord, but it's huge! Why have I never seen photographs
of it? Most old homesteads are well documented. Who on
earth lives there?'

'I do,' he told her, his voice very dry, 'and as it is my
house and I like privacy, no one photographs it unless
they take them from the sea.'

He was leaning against the dusty side of the Land
Rover, irony hardening those striking features as he
watched her. After the first astounded moment Finley
burst into laughter, shaking her head at him.

'Oh, you lucky, lucky devil! Do you wear ruffled shirts
with diamond studs?—and you should have a thin
moustache, and long, flexible fingers!'

'That,' he returned haughtily, amusement glinting
through his lashes, 'was the river-boat gambler, not the

plantation owner. Ruffled shirts! I'm far too large to wear anything but the plainest clothes.'

'Limiting, this size business, isn't it?' she agreed flippantly. 'The same thing applies to miniatures like me. One tiny ruffle and I look like a shipwreck, all tossing waves and flotsam. Tell me, is your house as incredible inside as it is out?'

'Sir James had far from Spartan tastes,' he punned, grinning at her horrified expression. 'Come and see.'

Well, that explained the imperturbable air of self-assurance. If Blake Caird owned Motuaroha he had to be rich beyond anyone she had ever encountered before. Vainly, she searched her brain for any information that she might have tucked away, and to her surprise came up with a name.

'Morgan Caird,' she said triumphantly.

'My cousin.' He slanted her a narrow glance, apparently knowing the route down to the homestead so well that he didn't need to watch ahead. 'Do you know him?'

Finley swallowed, only relaxing when his eyes were safely on the road once more. 'I've met him. I helped deliver his baby.'

The hard authority of his features softened. 'Ah, yes,' he said. 'Morgan was almost effusive with gratitude. I gather it was a rather protracted birth, and the man is besotted with his wife.'

'And she with him,' Finley said promptly. Her smile was reminiscent. Finley had liked the Cairds very much, almost envying them their absorption in each other. Their baby son, a delectable little replica of his father, had been welcomed into their magic circle; his welfare was assured. Finley thought of some of the children she had had to deal with, and sighed.

At her feet the spaniel shivered, pressing his nose into her leg. You and me both, she thought wryly, scratching the matted poll by her knee. We're both out of our element here, but it will be fun to visit for a while.

The gardens around the homestead were a subtropical fantasy, huge pohutukawa trees sheltering the brilliant flowers of crêpe myrtles and hibiscus, the enormous slashed leaves of fruit salad plants and the heavily scented blooms of gardenias and datura.

'They—you can't possibly grow coconuts here,' she said faintly, as they left the main drive for a strip of cobble-stones which led to the back of the house, irrepressible humour twinkling in the depths of her eyes. Of course, she would arrive at the tradesmen's entrance!

'They're a smaller, more hardy type,' he told her, 'and they flourish in our micro-climate. The only wind which gets into the bay is from the north, and that's hot and wet.'

'It's fantastic.'

Finley lifted dazzled eyes to meet the calm certitude in his. 'It's the only place I want to live in,' he said as he switched off the engine. 'I think I'd wither and die away from the island. Now, let's first have a look at this apology for an animal.'

An hour later the dog had been bathed and clipped free of matted hair, dosed and fed and watered, injected for every disease known to the canine world and put into a kennel with a large fenced run. He watched dubiously as Finley left but, beyond a whimper which soon tailed off, he seemed reconciled to losing his saviour. Somewhat bemused by Blake's expertise and the well-equipped veterinary clinic, Finley allowed herself to be escorted back to the house, seated in an extremely comfortable chair beneath a large flowering jacaranda tree and served with tea which he had made while she was washing her face and hands in a luxurious little powder-room not too far from the back door.

'You've been very kind,' she said, trying to overlook the appreciative gleam in those gold eyes as they rested on the slender shapeliness of her legs. 'I'm certain that if the dog realised what you have done for him he'd appreciate it too.'

The gleam warmed into laughter. 'All dogs back off when confronted by a needle,' he returned. 'I rather envied him. The way he buried his head in your bosom was extremely touching.'

'I do hope I'm not keeping you from something you should be doing.' She set her cup and saucer down with a little sharp sound.

'Nothing important,' he said, mocking her. 'Tell me about yourself.'

'There's nothing to tell.' Beneath the T-shirt her shoulders moved in a slight shrug.

Just above her head another cicada joined in the chorus, its shrill little anthem softened into music by the languorous ambience.

'What made you decide to be a doctor?'

'I never wanted to be anything else. I was about five when I made the decision.' Normally she wasn't particularly communicative, preferring to listen rather than to talk, but he was clever, he probed so tactfully that minutes later she realised that she had let him see far more than was wise; she felt as though she had been dissected by a master.

Stiffly, she said, 'But I must be boring you witless.'

'I never allow myself to be bored,' he told her, something like sarcasm colouring the deep tones. 'What about marriage? Don't you feel any need for a husband in this carefully planned life of yours?'

'You certainly believe in getting your pound of flesh, don't you? Yes, I'd like to get married, if it fits in.'

He lifted a dark brow. 'Been burned, Finley?'

Her smile was dazzling, meaningless. 'I've been engaged. It didn't work out.'

'Why?'

Small teeth clamped on to her bottom lip. She wanted to tell him to go to hell, to stop poking about in the corners of her mind, but she made the mistake of glancing up. The compelling demand in his eyes forced the truth from her.

'He was very ambitious, very clever. He wanted a wife who would provide back-up services while he clawed his way up the corporate ladder. He did not want a medical student who spent all her time studying and whose workload was going to get heavier the further she went. I am also incapable of whipping up a gourmet meal in fifteen minutes, and I tend to go to sleep when anyone talks business, even when that someone was Graeme's boss.'

'Can't you cook?'

She smiled tightly, still angry with him. 'Oh, I can manage a reasonable meal but to me *cuisine minceur* sounds like something to do with Sweeney Todd, and I simply can't be bothered standing for hours to concoct a sauce to go with the crayfish tails.'

He laughed and said, 'It's almost a relief to come across a woman who doesn't aspire to be a *cordon bleu* cook. Every young thing I meet seems to have spent half her life at various esoteric cookery courses. They drive my housekeeper crazy by offering to produce gourmet meals, all of which necessitate an immediate trip to the mainland for a vital ingredient.'

A caustic intonation raised her brows. He shrugged, and said, 'Life on the island can be dull if you're accustomed to the amenities of the mainland. The hotel doesn't compensate for the lack of choice.'

'Been burned, Blake?'

'Haven't we all?' His mouth compressed at an unpleasant memory.

Finley regretted the mocking little repetition of his own question but, after a quick glance at him, she

decided that her sympathy was misplaced. If anyone was
self-sufficient it was surely Blake Caird.

Something must have shown in her face because he
sent her a smile of such profound cynicism that she was
repelled.

'A marriage,' he elaborated without expression. 'The
isolation put paid to it.'

She frowned, impelled to offer some sort of sympathy
in spite of his lack of emotion. 'I'm sorry.'

'So am I.' He hesitated, the tough face suddenly
drawn. 'She drowned trying to escape.'

'Oh, my dear.' Finley was on her feet and beside him
without realising she had moved; she stooped, her hands
drawing the bright head to rest against her breast in the
age-old embrace of solace.

She could feel his astonishment as though it was
visible, yet when she began to pull away his arm snaked
about her waist.

'Stay there,' he said, and although there was surprise in
his voice there was wonder too. 'What branch of
medicine are you planning to specialise in?'

'Pediatrics.'

'I think you are going to be an excellent pediatrician.
You have a compassionate heart.'

She looked down at the gleam of his hair against the
gentle contours of her breasts. He moved, nuzzling, and
suddenly there was nothing maternal in what she was
offering and he accepting. The air, already humming
with the song of the cicadas, became charged and
sizzling with something else. Finley's hands tightened in
the warm crispness of his hair; his mouth moved against
her breast and a pang of exquisite sensation rippled
through her body. Slowly her hand slid down to the
heated skin of his neck, hesitated, then worked its way
beneath the collar of his shirt to find the strongly defined
bone of his shoulder.

He muttered something and pulled her between his knees. His hands almost spanned her waist; they contracted, clenching painfully and she bit her lip, a frown twitching her fine brows together.

His grip relaxed. His hands moved upwards under the thin cotton knit of her shirt, smoothing over her rib-cage. He was smiling, drooping lids failing to hide the gold which flamed up into fire as the harsh features clamped into an expression as old as humanity, the urgency of desire.

Finley's knees buckled. Instantly she was swept on to his lap. One lean hand took immediate advantage and moved higher, cupping her breast with delicate, erotic precision.

A sudden explosion of her senses dragged a stifled moan from lips which were clumsy and stiff. A deep breath hurt her lungs. When his mouth found the bubbling pulse in the hollow of her throat she was wracked by tremors. Blindly, every instinct urging her towards the one inevitable conclusion, she rested her cheek on the wheat-bright head, breathing in the erotic, indefinable scent of his masculinity while tides of sensation surged through her body.

Passion seemed irresistible, a vital, necessary progression, but, although his knowing hands and mouth compelled response, Finley knew that she had to call a halt while she had enough command of herself to do it.

He seemed not to notice when she straightened. His mouth clung, tasting the soft silk of her throat. Gently, both hands trembling, she cradled his head, fighting to repress the incandescent desire he had aroused.

He was too experienced to miss her withdrawal. He whispered something short and savage against her skin and lifted his head to search her face. For a long moment, until the flames in his eyes died and they became enigmatically amber again, she thought that such an intense scrutiny must see through the veil of flesh to the essential person beneath.

Then he smiled, crookedly, and she moved free of him to a sensible distance away.

'Not that sort of woman, Finley?' The words were slightly slurred, but he was once more in control.

She reacted to the sardonic tone with an unconscious lift of her head. 'Sorry, I don't make a habit of sleeping with anyone within a few hours of meeting them.'

'You'd rather offer comfort than yourself.' He rose, making full use of his height to stare her down, his eyes suddenly as piercing as shards of golden glass. Unexpectedly they warmed and he said, 'Perhaps you're wise.'

'It's safer that way, and I'm a cautious person.'

His expression was a masterpiece of aloof irony with the warning barely hidden. 'So am I, usually. I believe that only an idiot allows himself to get burned twice.'

He could hardly have made it more plain. Like him, Finley had no intention of embarking on any sort of affair, but it was going to be difficult to banish the intrusive images which had danced in her mind, tempting her so that for a few mad moments she had almost abandoned the considered decision she had made in adolescence, and reaffirmed several times since then. And it was not going to be easy to forget the heavy, heated reaction of her body to his touch.

CHAPTER TWO

LATER, in the impersonal luxury of her hotel bedroom, Finley tried to analyse exactly why that cynical statement should have so depressed her. Rather dauntingly for one who prided herself on her caution, she discovered that it was because it underlined his determination not to embark on anything more binding than an affair.

'Although why that should depress you, heaven knows,' she told her reflection severely. 'Unless it's that virgins of twenty-six have these romantic hangovers from adolescence.'

Then, of course, she had believed that you could have it all, an absorbing career, a grand passion leading to a happy marriage, babies—the sort of life only those with the blinkered eyes of youth could dream of. She was more sensible now. It was simply a matter of choices. You made your choices and then you lived with the results. And the circumstances of her broken engagement had revealed to her that it was as necessary for her to follow her vocation as it was for her to breathe. If she married, her husband was going to have to accept that.

Experience had also taught her that grand passion was only another name for a violent physical attraction, and that whatever else it led to, marriage was not often on the agenda. And when it was, it was usually a disaster.

Blake had behaved honourably by making it clear that an affair was what he had in mind. No doubt, when his dynastic urge asserted itself he would marry some nice girl from his own level of society who would find fulfilment in being his wife, the chatelaine of that beautiful house, and bearing little Cairds. Almost certainly they would be very happy together.

And so would she, with or without a husband, or lover, or children.

She would have liked to have seen over the house. By unspoken agreement he had driven her back to the hotel immediately after that embrace, his pleasant courteous mask failing to hide the fact that he had retreated to some aloof region of his mind to which she was definitely not admitted. She had thanked him for taking responsibility for the dog; he had replied that she had no need to worry any further about it, he would see that it went to a good and loving home.

It was goodbye and they both knew it was the only sensible thing to do, but, just as she had turned to leave him, he had touched a strand of the chocolate-coloured hair which flowed over her shoulder. Her eyes enormous and shadowed, she had watched as he lifted it to his lips.

Then he had bent and kissed her, lifting his head too soon but still leaving an exotic taste of masculinity on her unsatisfied mouth.

'Nice to have met you,' he said softly, his expression completely impassive, and she had said goodbye in a surprisingly firm voice before walking straight-backed into the hotel, not daring to look round.

Now, in retrospect, it seemed rather silly. She had behaved like a girl with her first crush, all drama and sensation, and he had backed off.

Very sensible. But she couldn't help wondering just what it would be like to be initiated by him into the rapturous world of sensuality. Mind-shattering, she thought with hollow flippancy, as more unwanted images seared into her brain. They persisted, even after she had gone down to dinner, so she was glad when the waiter showed two people to her table, both swathed in the unmistakable aura of honeymooners, both offering her tentative smiles while the waiter stood behind with the huffy expression of a man whose good advice has been ignored.

'You looked a bit lonely,' the girl said, 'But if you don't want company we'll get the waiter to find us another table.'

Not very easily, the dining-room was full. So, although Finley usually enjoyed her solitary state, she couldn't resist what seemed close to a plea, and smiled a welcome.

They had arrived three days before and although neither of them said so, it appeared that they felt a little out of their element.

'Mark helped build some additions on to the hotel,' his bride informed Finley, 'and he decided then that we'd spend our honeymoon here. It's lovely, isn't it?'

Finley agreed, feeling suddenly immensely older than the five or so years which separated them. She listened to details of the wedding, enjoying the bride's practical outlook, and heard about Mark's new job on one of the big office blocks across the harbour in Auckland. They discussed fashion and one or two of the less controversial issues of the day, found an acquaintance in common, and Finley heard of their desire to travel.

Well pleased with themselves and each other, they ate their meal and adjourned to the lounge for coffee.

'They've certainly poured money into this place,' Mark observed as he added his third spoonful of sugar to his cup. 'When you think that five years ago it was just a bay with a few pohutukawa trees and some cattle! But all it takes is money, isn't it? I suppose if you've got as much as Blake Caird you don't have to worry about spending a lot to get a lot. He owns the rest of the island too, his family's been here for donkey's years. Quite a guy.'

'Oh, you say that because he's taller than you!' The bride exchanged a smile with her husband before sending a woman to woman look in Finley's direction. 'Not that I've seen him, but when Mark was working here he used to see him and his wife quite often. All the women were after him even though he was married.'

'Wasn't interested,' Mark explained. 'Well, stands to reason. His wife was the best looking woman I've ever seen. Beautiful, like a model or a film star. They looked like something out of television together. Mind you, we saw more of her than him. She spent a lot of time dining and dancing, she liked a good time.' It was easy to see that he didn't understand how Blake Caird could neglect his wife so. He finished rather defiantly. 'We didn't see much of him at all.'

'It was terrible, the way she died.' The bride's expression sharpened into the avidity of a true gossip. 'It was an awful storm and she went out in one of their launches and ran on to the rocks on a point on the other side. At the inquest it came out that they'd had a fight and she was hysterical and he'd locked her in their bedroom, but she'd got out somehow and taken off. All because she wanted to go to a party! She must have been off her head with temper to be so stupid.'

'She was a redhead,' Mark agreed, as if that explained it. Finley was appalled. 'How terrible,' she said woodenly, remembering the bleak cynicism in Blake's expression when he spoke of the woman who had found his lovely home to be a prison.

'Just goes to show that money and looks don't give you everything,' the bride said comfortably. 'I don't know that I blame her, really. This place is all very nice in summer, but just imagine what it must be like in winter, cut off for days on end——'

Her husband laughed. 'Oh, come on, Vicki, it's not as bad as that! It'd take a pretty fierce storm to cut the place off at all, and certainly not for days on end. This is sheltered water, not the roaring forties.'

'Well, *I* wouldn't like to live so far from the shops,' Vicki declared.

Shortly after, they left to dance. Finley drank another cup of coffee, assuaging her guilt with the knowledge that even if it did keep her awake half the night she could sleep in the next day, then made her way up to bed.

It had, she decided as she undressed, been a pretty full day, and although it was only shortly after nine she was exhausted.

She was woken by the discordant burr of the telephone from the restless sleep which heralds true awakening. As she groped for the receiver she was haunted by fragments of a dream about a red-haired woman who ran screaming from a tall blond man.

Blake's voice seemed a continuation of the nightmare; she winced, shivering back under the sheet.

'What do you want?' Her voice was husky, the words curt to the point of rudeness.

'You. Your dog is refusing to eat—or stop howling,' he informed her grimly.

'Oh dear, I'm so sorry——' The dream fled, to be replaced by a guilt no less strong for being quite irrational.

He laughed. 'Yes, you might well be sorry! We've not had a restful night here. I'll pick you up in half an hour.'

'Hey—just wait a minute, I——'

'Don't worry about breakfast. Half an hour,' he repeated inexorably, and hung up.

Finley was ready, dressed in a bitter green cotton sundress which made the most of her flawless skin and long legs. As she came into the foyer she saw him listening to the manager of the hotel, that same Mike Cloud who was a sucker for a pretty face.

Finley waited a little distance away, not wanting to break into what seemed to be a serious conversation. She found herself wondering what it was beside his height and build that made Blake stand out so. The man with him was almost as tall, and better looking, but it was his companion who was attracting the attention. Sheer, total animal magnetism, she decided as Blake looked across and saw her. He possessed a virile, assured sexuality which showed in every inch of his powerful predator's body. And in his smile, and in the amber glitter of his eyes as they met hers.

'Good morning,' he said softly as they met.

Finley stiffened at the knowing look which escaped the manager as he was introduced to her, but he was pleasant enough and she forgave him for his assumption. Perhaps Blake was in the habit of choosing his bed-mates from the hotel register. Hardly fastidious, but then, men were strange creatures. At that moment a woman, elegant and provocative in a sleek sun-dress, walked by, her cleverly made-up eyes fixed on Blake with conscious invitation, and Finley realised that perhaps the manager had reason for his judgement of her. Blake appeared not to notice the blatant welcome in the other woman's languid movements, and in her pose as she paused a little further on, but he had seen her. And who, Finley thought, trying to hide an unseemly jealousy with charity, could blame him if he accepted an occasional such invitation?

'I hope,' Blake said belatedly as he slid into the Land Rover beside her, 'that you didn't have plans for today.'

'None whatsoever. While I'm here I have no intention of doing anything but laze around and perfect my tan. Blake, I'm so sorry about the dog. Did he howl all night?'

'No.' But as she smiled her relief he continued, 'Not after midnight. That's when I finally succumbed and took him into my bedroom. From then on he just whimpered.'

'Oh, Lord!' She met his teasing sideways glance with a plea. 'You are joking, aren't you?'

'Sorry.'

'But what am I going to do? If he's going to carry on

like that not even the kindest home will want him, and I don't think it would be fair to him if I kept him. He'd be alone such a lot. Being a good Samaritan,' she finished gloomily, 'is not all it's cracked up to be.'

'You could come and stay with me,' he suggested reasonably. 'By the end of your holiday you may be able to come up with some idea. He will probably have calmed down a little by then, too. I imagine he's having the canine version of a nervous breakdown. He should recover fairly quickly, spaniels are essentially cheerful dogs.'

Finley opened her mouth, thought better of her first impetuous refusal and began again, sedately. 'That's very kind of you——'

'Nonsense. I happen to need six hours' sleep at least, and so do my employees. So, presumably, do the guests at the hotel, which I happen to own. So you can't keep him there. If the guests are driven away and the staff made inefficient through lack of sleep, I stand to lose a quite substantial slice of my income. It's in my interest to offer you a room until you go.'

He spoke in such a reasonable tone that Finley almost accepted the pompous little speech as serious until she caught the betraying quiver of a muscle beside that stern mouth. A crow of laughter escaped her.

'How very sensible you make it sound,' she said, still laughing, 'but you can't possibly want me.'

There followed an odd little silence during which she had time to reflect on a choice of words which could have been more felicitous, before he replied smoothly, 'Of course I don't, but I shall endeavour to hide my chagrin at being forced to endure your company.'

She said wistfully, 'I should go home, I suppose.'

'According to this morning's weather report Auckland is suffering from one of its spells of high humidity.'

'Oh, dear.' She knew well what that meant. Sticky days

and unbearable nights.

'Exactly. Not good weather for a convalescent. Mike promised to have your clothes packed and they'll be following us shortly, so I suggest you brace yourself for a reunion with the dog.'

Which left Finley with nothing to say.

'I can be quite an amiable companion,' he told her kindly, after some moments of rather hunted silence on her part. 'And when you get bored you can always head back to the hotel for a few hours of civilisation.'

The flick of glacial contempt in the even voice made Finley wince. Last night's gossip seemed written on her face; she didn't have to know him more than she did to understand how humiliating he must find the whispered rumours about his wife's death. He was, she thought, a very proud man. It would have been salt in the wound of his grief.

She gazed steadfastly through the windscreen at the brilliant day, radiant with the blue and green and gold of high summer, and tried hard to ignore the flare of excitement deep within her.

'The grass looks in good condition.' she remarked, tacitly accepting his invitation to stay. 'I suppose all that rain in the spring helped.'

'It did, as has the fact that we've had at least an inch every week so far this summer. And very little wind. It's been an exceptionally good season.'

'You must suffer in a drought.'

He nodded, lean hands relaxed and competent at the wheel as the road dived back down a gully. 'A week without rain constitutes a drought. Coastal country dries out quickly.'

'How do you deal with it?'

'There are dams all over the island and I've sunk several bores. I irrigate, grow tree lucerne which sends roots metres down into the soil and can stand up to most droughts. As a last resort, I barge stock over to the mainland.'

'Do you have a run-off there?'

'Yes,' he said after the slightest of hesitations. 'The main thing, of course, is not to over-stock. At the beginning of each summer I quit as much stock as I think desirable.'

Until she was ten, Finley had lived in a small country town in the Waikato. That had been dairying country but she had carried an interest in all things rural to the city with her, so she continued to ask questions, many displaying an ignorance she made no attempt to hide. Blake answered briefly but informatively, occasionally teasing her at her lack of knowledge. And all around, seen from high on the hills and at sea level between a screen of pohutukawa trees, the Hauraki gulf glittered in a peacock display so brilliant it hurt to look straight at it.

'What about deer?' Finley asked rather desperately, because the sparkle of the water seemed to have invaded her bloodstream and she felt as though she was drunk on pleasure.

'Deer?'

Once more there was that reserve she had noticed before. Finley shook hair back from a suddenly heated cheek. 'Aren't farmers diversifying into deer now? And Angora goats? I'm sure that I read that up north they sold a flock of Angora goats for incredibly high prices.'

'Stupidly high,' he asserted, 'but the principle is a good one. Our future lies in diversification.'

Beneath them a cattle-stop rattled a noisy greeting. Finley looked eagerly about as they drove past the buildings and equipment needed for a large agricultural enterprise. It was like a small village, a resemblance strengthened when the road passed a cluster of houses by the beach, a horse paddock, and a small building.

'Is that a school?'

'Yes.' Blake waved to a man seated on a massive tractor, then slowed down to avoid an over-excited cat which streaked in front of the Land Rover. 'We've just added another room. Several of the permanent staff at the hotel have families and the roll is rising.'

'It's a long walk from the hotel to here.'

'They come by school bus.'

'It's just like a village.'

'Like a very small village,' he said crisply, as he turned the wheel to take the road up to the homestead. 'One with large gaps in the array of amenities people have come to consider essential. It's only since the hotel was built that we've had mains power, and in winter there are days when you can stand on top of the highest hill and taste the salt spray, and at night the lights on the mainland seem as far away as heaven.'

Had he grown to hate his wife? No, hate was probably too strong a word, but it must be her memory which iced his voice with contempt. He sounded as though in the end all he had been able to do was despise her.

Finley's lashes drooped to hide her pity.

As the engine was switched off a high, forlorn wailing assaulted her ears. 'He sounds so miserable,' she said, jumping out.

He looked miserable, too. He was tied to a chair surrounded by various tempting titbits ranging from a bone to a slice of cheese, not one of which was touched. A bowl of water to one side was also untouched. Watching the intruder with unwinking interest were three large cats. The howling stopped when he saw Finley, but his thin body began to tremble, and he hurled himself at her until the leash brought him up short and he skidded into the bowl of water.

'Poor old love,' Finley crooned, kneeling to cuddle the bedraggled, quivering animal. It took a while before the frightened, ecstatic dog calmed down under the influence of her endearments and petting hand, but at last he did.

'See if he'll eat now,' Blake suggested from his vantage point of a few yards away.

He did, keeping a watchful eye on his goddess as he gulped down everything in his line of sight. The cats eyed him with disgust as he almost drained the water, wetting his ears profusely, and when he shook himself they stalked off like offended dowagers, leaving him in clear possession of the field. Finley's amused glance met Blake's, but neither spoke until the dog sighed and sat down firmly on Finley's feet.

'This is ridiculous!' She looked in half laughing dismay from his shaggy, satisfied face, up and up into Blake's suddenly severe countenance and fell silent, reading there the same desire which had flamed between them yesterday: naked, almost impersonal, the hard lines of his face stripped of everything but a fierce consuming hunger.

Fear shook her, and excitement, and an answering need so intense that she went white with the effort to control it.

How long they stood frozen in a tableau of mute passion she never knew. Probably it was only a few seconds, yet it seemed that in those moments she became another person.

A voice interrupted, a pleasant female voice which came from just inside the door.

'Well, that's a relief,' it said, and resolved itself into an extremely attractive woman in her mid-thirties, clad in a large white apron, a cotton shirt, and shorts. Finley blinked, trying hard to get a grip on herself.

'Ah, Phil.' Blake's deep tones were amused as he introduced his housekeeper.

'Believe me, we're all glad to see you,' Phil Allen said pleasantly. 'He was beginning to upset the children.'

She smiled, but there was little warmth in it.

'Oh dear,' Finley muttered, wondering why Blake's housekeeper mistrusted her. On her feet the dog shifted fractionally; he was warm and heavy and she could feel the movements of his tail as it wagged. 'See what you've got me into,' she complained. 'I spend all my time apologising for your behaviour and I don't even know you!'

Not at all abashed he sneezed politely and the tail increased its tempo.

'Come and wash your hands,' Blake commanded. 'Breakfast on the terrace, Phil?'

'Yes, it's ready.'

It was delicious, fresh fish served with dill and lemon slices, hash browns, crisp white melon adorned with late strawberries, and coffee so removed from the instant blend Finley normally drank, that she wondered if it came from the same bush. On a leaf in the middle of the table a huge hibiscus rested in satiny gold and scarlet flamboyance, bees hummed with purposeful industry in the thyme and rosemary at the edge of the terrace and, blended with the scent of the herbs and the coffee, was another, aphrodisiac perfume which floated across on the warm air from the velvet flowers of a gardenia.

'You live,' Finley said extravagantly, 'in the most perfect place on earth.'

'At this moment. It palls quickly, I understand.'

Well, she didn't care if he thought all women found life in his small paradise boring and dull after a few months. If he wasn't able to appreciate that his wife had perhaps been a shallow woman unable to cope with the reality of life 'so far from the shops' Finley certainly wasn't going to try to convince him.

She flashed him a brilliant smile and said airily. 'As I'm never likely to see it in the depths of winter, I'll keep all my illusions spendidly intact. At this moment, I think Motuaroha could give the Garden of Eden points and come out the winner.'

A brow lifted in silent mockery but he made no obvious quip about the resident snake; instead he pointed out a huge cruise liner which was making its way into the channel which led to the Waitemata harbour and Auckland. While she was watching it through a pair of binoculars Phil Allen came to tell him that someone wanted to see him. After he had excused himself and left, the housekeeper asked if she could get Finley anything else.

'No, thank you, that was superb.'

'Thank you.'

The woman's reticence struck her as a little chilly, but Finley would not allow herself to be affected by it. If she was going to leave the island with her heart intact she was going to have to glide along on the surface of life here. No involvement, and above all no indulgence in the kind of sensual combat which had so alarmed her yesterday and this morning. Clearly, Blake would be happy enough to welcome her into his bed. She did not need experience to tell her that an affair with him would be immensely exciting. And, ultimately, devastating.

If she had any foresight, she would be fleeing back to the mainland as fast as she could go. But that, she thought with bravado, would be cowardly, and if she was sensible she would come to no harm. And one thing she was rather proud of was her common sense.

Firmly repressing images which lurked just below her level of consciousness and seemed only too eager to emerge into the light, Finley asked if she could help with the dishes.

'No, thank you.' The housekeeper was very firm. 'Why don't you wait here until Blake gets back? He shouldn't be too long. It will take that cruise liner quite a while to pass us.'

'A good idea.' Finley watched with grave, considering

eyes as the older woman cleared the table. When she had gone, she walked, the dog half a pace behind, across the bricks and down wide, shallow steps to the lawn. A late-rising blackbird, shrieking loudly, flew into the spreading branches of the jacaranda. Finley held her face up to the sun, smiling as the warmth washed deliciously over her.

Not for the first time, she wondered why she was so adamant in her refusal to join the sexual revolution. Partly it had been because she had had intimate knowledge of the casualties it left behind, and her medical training had only reinforced that early experience. But she knew another reason, now. Simply, it was that she had never met a man who aroused her enough to make the risks worthwhile. It was her misfortune that it was Blake Caird who possessed the key to the passion which slept within her, because there was no future for them. Her life was with her profession, and she would be unable to practise it here, where his life was.

'You should be ashamed of yourself,' she grumbled at the dog. 'Here I am in danger to life and limb, not to mention chastity, and all because of you. What's your name anyway?'

She sat down on the short grass and began to reel off syllables, hoping to get some response which might indicate his name. Head tilted to one side, his tail making rapid sweeps, he watched her with blackberry eyes while she chanted a series of sounds at him.

A low noise, more like a purr than a growl, and the refocusing of the dog's eyes to a point above and behind Finley, indicated Blake's arrival. She hadn't heard a thing; for such a big man he moved with a surprising lack of noise.

'I think,' she informed him a little breathlessly, 'that his name is something like Black. See, he gets quite excited when I say it. Black, here Black . . .'

'Blackie.'

'Of course!' The spaniel was sitting up alertly, its gaze switching from one to the other, its hindquarters moving in a frenzy of pleasure.

'Hardly original,' Finley said, loftily.

'No, but descriptive. Now that we know who he is, would you like to come for a drive with me? I have to check out a fence line.'

Finley allowed herself to be helped to her feet, but she delayed their departure by a little tug on the hand which enveloped hers. Obediently, he halted those long panther strides and looked down into her earnest face, his brows lifting quizzically.

'You don't have to feel that you must keep me entertained,' she told him. 'I realise this is a complete imposition on you and I—well, I'm very grateful. I'll be more than happy to lie inconspicuously in the sun and be as unobtrusive as possible.'

He grinned and ran a lean forefinger down her straight nose. Only the teasing glint in his eyes gave the lie to the solemnity of his words. 'Somehow I don't think you could be inconspicuous. You haven't the face or the figure for it. My mother would have said that you have style.'

That was all, an offhand compliment delivered with throw-away charm, yet the effect on Finley was astounding. Counteracting a heated dizziness the only way she could, she pulled free and stepped back. The teasing amusement vanished; watching the gold in his eyes flame up into incandescence, she realised that she had hurtled headfirst into a situation she couldn't handle.

Yet even as awareness sparkled with ruthless intensity between them, she saw an ironic understanding in his expression, the hint of fellow feeling which drew her as much as the primitive call of male to female.

'You make me nervous,' she stammered.

He chuckled at that, deep in his throat. 'You

encourage the hunter in me.'

'That sounds chauvinistic, and cruel.'

Again that lift of one dark brow, giving his face a hard sardonic cast. 'All men are hunters at heart, didn't you know? The act of love itself can be many things, but basically it is a ritual of surrender and submission, mastery and triumph, for both participants. Courtship is a formalised pattern of the chase and the end is inevitable, death of a sort. Some call it the little death, some satiation. But it's the closest we come on earth to the ecstasies of paradise—or of hell. So if you see yourself as prey, little doctor, you're right.'

Appalled by such cynicism she said, 'If that's what you really believe, it's no wonder your wife left you!'

The hasty words resounded like the crack of a rifle, shattering the peace, splintering in the still sweet air like jagged missiles. Finley froze.

With eyes as flat and emotionless as pebbles he said, 'That is none of your business.'

'No,' she said, shaken and ashamed, 'and I shouldn't have said that. I didn't mean it. But, although I don't believe in the kind of romantic slush that often passes for love—a sentimental veil over the urge to mate—I've seen plenty of good marriages between people who like and respect each other too much to go in for the sort of attitudes you described.'

'You're an expert on the dynamics of marriage?'

'I don't even know what that means,' she said, much too sweetly. 'But I have friends, and I'd know if their marriages were basically as rotten as that. When there are shared interests and compatibility a marriage has a pretty good base.'

'And love?' he asked, still with the same derisive note in his voice.

She shrugged. 'What's love? Ask a hundred people and

you get a hundred different definitions. I think love comes afterwards.'

'You are a greater cynic than I am.' His half closed eyes searched her intense little face. 'I at least allow for passion. Your idea of the perfect marriage sounds like the bloodless affection of close friends!'

'And yours sounds like the coupling of a pair of tigers I once saw on television. Short, vicious, and bloody, with no emotion expended and none expected. No doubt it was pleasurable for the participants, but it was really just the instinctive surrender to a basic drive.'

The air seemed to throb about her, the sizzle of the cicadas sawing at her nerves. He was still watching her with a taunting appreciation which stripped her of humanity to reduce her to a set of female characteristics; it was degrading and familiar. She should be accustomed by now to men who judged her solely by her fragile prettiness. Some found it impossible to accept her as a competent doctor. Why feel betrayed because Blake Caird was no more perceptive?

But she should not have said what she had; her temper had propelled her across an invisible boundary, one fenced about with 'No Trespassers' signs. It was a forbidden border and behind it danger stalked in the lithe, soundless steps of the man before her.

For a tense moment she thought he was going to free the danger from its leash. An emotion too fierce for containment burned in his gaze until, with a restraint which made her shiver because there was something inhuman in it, he mastered it. As mildly as if they had been discussing a book, he said, 'We'll just have to disagree. My offer of a trip into the hills stands. We won't be away for long and I'd enjoy your company.'

Which was sweet of him, for a more self-sufficient man it would be hard to imagine. Finley nodded and said, 'Yes, I'd love to see your island. Thank you.'

Ten minutes later they were driving over one of the well maintained roads towards the island's highest point and she was following his conversational lead. It was easy enough. His quick, perceptive mind made him an intriguing companion. They talked of rock-climbing and the best way to train a mature dog, of the known history of the Maori tribe that had carefully sculptured several of the hills into fortresses.

He told her anecdotes of life on the island, choosing ones so outrageous that she retaliated with some of her more hilarious experiences as a medical student.

CHAPTER THREE

'YOU'VE never considered going into general practice?'

'No.' Her voice expressed a serene confidence which refused any other possibility.

Blake guided the Land Rover up the last, steepest incline, pulled in under a tree and cut the engine. Hands still on the wheel he leaned forward, looking at the slope before them through eyes narrowed against the glare of sun and sea. His tanned forearms contrasted blatantly with the faded checked shirt he was wearing. Finley watched as his hands relaxed. Long-fingered and strong—in spite of the manual work he did, they were well cared for, the nails clipped and clean.

'I knew what I wanted to do when I was about five,' she said, using the words to suppress a tantalising image of those hands on the white skin of her breasts. 'My mother used to say that even when I was a baby I never cried when I was immunised, I was too interested in what was going on. But when I was five I fell out of a tree and cut my knee badly enough to need attention.' Absently, her finger caressed the scar, barely visible now in the satiny skin above her knee.

'And?'

Somewhat self-consciously she grinned. 'I can remember it so vividly. I was absolutely fascinated. I sat bug-eyed while it was cleaned and sutured and, after that, I used to slip off down to the surgery whenever I could. The doctor was very good, although I must have been the most incredible nuisance. He even tried to convince my parents that my interest in blood and gore wasn't abnormal. I'm afraid his efforts were in vain.'

He leaned back in his seat, dropping a hand over hers

as it traced the scar. His finger stroking her skin was the most erotic thing that had ever happened to her. A sharp stab of sensation at the base of her spine followed by a strange melting heat between her thighs made her catch her breath. She could not drag her hand away from beneath his. Unmoving, she sat scanning his remote, abstracted profile with wild eyes.

At last, speaking huskily through the bubble which threatened to block her throat, she finished, 'Then we moved away, and for years I got no closer to a surgery than the front gate. I was a very healthy child. But I knew what I was going to be.'

'Why did you move away?'

The sun beat down on to the baking ground. Below them, from a gully green with the remnants of the native bush which had once covered the island, the song of the cicadas rose in shrill cadences. Finley swallowed, looking back down the years to that first betrayal, that first wound to the spirit.

'My parents divorced,' she told him bleakly. 'My father was a stock agent, he had to go where he was sent, and of course, that meant living in the country. He enjoyed small-town life. My mother liked shops and theatres and her family and friends in Auckland. There was probably more to it than that, but that was how they explained it to me.'

Strangely, in spite of the sensuous effect of his touch on her skin, she felt a kind of comfort in it.

'Tough,' he said, and lifted his hand to cup her cheek for a moment before removing it entirely.

She hid her reaction with a shrug. 'I got over it. Given time you can get over anything.'

'A stoic, I see,' he teased, swooping to drop a quick kiss on her startled mouth. 'One with an altogether too enticing mouth. We had better get something done about this fence before I get side-tracked. Put this hat on, you'll burn out there.'

It had been hot enough in the Land Rover, but the heat outside was like an evil emanation, swallowing her up in its fiery breath. Finley gasped at its strength and thanked him for thinking of a hat. She had seen enough skin cancer to make her very conscious of what New Zealand's sun could do to unprotected skin. Blackie, too, appeared intimidated by the heat. He sniffed around for a few moments before joining the other two dogs in the shade beneath the vehicle.

'Coward,' Finley taunted softly.

'They're too sensible to sit in the sun when they could be in the shade.' Blake spoke abstractedly; he was frowning at a concrete post in the fence which had snapped clean in half. As Finley watched he opened the boot and pulled out another post, hoisting it on to his shoulder.

'Can I help?' she asked, tentatively.

'You can bring the spade.'

There were several interesting-looking implements so she carried them all across, staggering slightly because as well as being heavy they were awkward. Before she had trailed half-way to the fence he had returned and, frowning, relieved her of them.

'Don't be stupid,' he said curtly. 'Sit down in the shade of that tree.'

Meekly, because it had been a stupid thing to do, she obeyed, curving her arms around her legs as she rested her chin on her knees.

Mending a fence involved several steps, all of them hard work. Finley watched with respect as he dug the snapped base free of earth which was compacted enough to make the spade ring slightly each time it was thrust into the ground. After five minutes his shirt was wringing wet, clinging to his torso so that the flexion of each muscle was clearly visible.

Finley felt a return of the strange pang of need deep
within her and swallowed, then began naming every
muscle, trying with the exercise to rid her mind of the
image of him naked and gleaming, a bronze warrior. It
seemed he was determined to frustrate such a praise-
worthy aim; he pulled his shirt over his head and she
bit her lip and looked away because the reality was
infinitely more disturbing than anything her imagination
was able to produce.

Lord, but he was *big*! Tanned skin gleaming with
sweat, the muscles moving in a rhythm of power and
endurance, he was so profoundly masculine that he
roused all that was feminine in her. For the first time
ever, she abandoned herself wholly to a sensuous
daydream.

Beneath her lashes her eyes gleamed green as a cat's.
The corners of her mouth lifted in a bland, unconscious
smile, as old as Lilith. Strange tides were flowing through
her body, rendering her languid, while her eyes remained
fixed in an unwinking stare on the powerful contours of
his torso, the play of energy in the long, heavily muscled
thighs, the formidable vigour of his movements.

Twice her tongue ran the length of her dry lips and still
she watched him, hands tightly clenched to stop the
trembling which seemed to originate deep within her
bones. Oh, but he was magnificent, and she wanted him
as she had never wanted another man, with a devouring
hunger which could easily overwhelm her if she let it.

Unaware of that level, avid gaze, Blake set the new
post in place, one hand holding it upright as he rammed
in earth around the butt. His corded arm rose and fell in a
regular rhythm which was an outward expression of the
kind of strength which awed her.

On the periphery of her vision a fantail flirted; its
high-pitched cheeping didn't impinge. Nor did the green
and brown grasshopper which landed clumsily on the
arch of her foot. She wasn't aware of its thoughtful

survey, or the fact that it flew off again after a few seconds. Beneath the Land Rover the dogs' sleep was punctuated by an occasional 'clop' as one snapped at a fly. The sun shone down with brazen ferocity, killing the faint breeze. Still Finley watched as Blake did things with wire and finally straightened up, the implements he had used hoisted in one smooth movement over his shoulder.

'Stay there,' he commanded when Finley recovered sufficiently from her sensual trance to begin to scramble to her feet.

She subsided back on to the dry grass as he deposited his load into the back of the vehicle and pulled out a small insulated bag.

'Here,' he said, dropping on to the ground beside her.

The bag contained a flask of babaco juice, sweetly acid and scented, and some superb scones, as well as a thermos of tea.

Finley poured tea, black and sugarless, but not, she was pleased to see, too strong, and he drank it quickly, every nerve stretched and alert. Although he had pulled his shirt back on she could not forget the polished, gleaming body beneath nor banish the salty, slightly musky scent of his physical effort from her nostrils. Lust, she told herself sternly, ignoring the beads of sweat which gathered at her temples and across her nose.

'Another cup?'

He didn't smile at her ridiculously formal tone, merely proffered his mug. He drank this one a little more slowly, while she tried the yellow babaco juice and forced her over-active sensory system into restraint. When he had finished he leaned back against the tree-trunk and exhaled in satisfaction, his eyes fixed on the panorama beneath them.

It was worth looking at. The island fell in folds and gathers and steep inclines to a sea of silver-blue enamel. Across it other islands floated in a light summer haze, insubstantial as dreams, the verdant growth of spring and early summer giving way to crisp gold pasture.

The main holiday season was over and the enormous fleet of yachts had dwindled, but still, everywhere the eye fell there were sails, many traditional white, more the pure, glowing colours of modern technology.

By turning her head Finley could see Rangitoto, the most recent island volcano in the isthmus, whose first eruption had laid down a deposit of fertile ash on Motuaroha. Behind it Auckland gleamed, a white city between its harbours. The mainland looked like a fairy realm glimpsed through the mists of fantasy, unreal, beyond reach. Behind them, the great bulk of Moehu brooded over the Coromandel peninsula and the Firth of Thames, a mountain blue as grapes in the summer haze.

'I've seen a fair amount of the world,' Blake said, 'and there's never been a view to equal this one.'

The calm, matter-of-fact words could not hide his total identification with this place. Finley hoped her startled curiosity didn't show as she said, 'You sound as though you hated to be away from it.'

The wide shoulders shifted slightly. 'I spent most of the time between ten and twenty-two away. Boarding school, university, working in America, a year's wandering in Europe. When I came back I decided that I was never going to leave again. So I've stayed put.' He turned his head, keeping her uncomfortably pinned under his steady gaze. 'This is my home. Although Motuaroha is not my only responsibility, and I spend quite a lot of time away from it, I sometimes think that I am only happy when I'm here.'

'You're very lucky,' she said slowly, shaken by the depth of feeling in the deep voice.

'Lucky?' He smiled with savage irony. 'Sometimes, I think it's a curse. Idolatry of any sort is a sin, and we pay for our sins. Only fair, I suppose, but occasionally others pay for them too. I don't suppose the man you were engaged to was happy when you jilted him for your vocation?'

'No.'

'We're two of a kind,' he said, shocking her with his arrogant certainty. 'Perhaps we lack some essential part of humanity. My world is more important to me than love ever could be and you—well, you don't even believe in love, do you?'

He had made her sound a freak, yet honesty forced her to admit the basic correctness of his conclusion. She shook her head but her acceptance must have shown, as well as her reluctance, for he laughed a little mockingly and hooked a powerful arm over her shoulder, pulling her so that her back came to rest against his chest.

'Sit still,' he said over her protests. 'Unless you find me unattractive to be near?'

He was actually concerned! She stopped wriggling and relaxed. 'I don't mind honest sweat—blood smells worse—but you're hot.'

'While you are as cool and sweet as the gardenias in my garden,' he murmured into the top of her head. 'Soft and scented, with a hint of lemon, and as fragile as a blossom. I feel that if I touch you I might mark that velvety skin.'

She tried to break the spell of his seductive wooing by saying acidly, 'As it happens, I have very strong walls to all of my blood vessels. You'd have to pinch quite hard to bruise me.'

She felt rather than heard his chuckle. 'Pinching was not exactly what I had in mind, my heart.'

The caressing endearment was strangely sweet. Almost sweet enough for her to respond provocatively by asking exactly what he *did* have in mind. Only her knowledge that he would tell her, and watch her reaction with that knowing smile, kept her silent.

But she wanted to set him right on one thing. 'You're wrong when you say I don't believe in love. I have seen the most incredible devotion . . . Only a fool would say that it doesn't exist. I believe that it's foolish to view passion through rose-tinted glasses. Love has to be earned. Even maternal love, which must be about the most intense, needs a growing period. A mother doesn't automatically love her baby.'

'And some never get there. It's just as well you're not going to be here for long. You have a talent for deflection.'

'Oh, yes?'

The wall of his chest behind her lifted and fell as he laughed beneath his breath. 'What a forbidding voice! All I had in mind was a little light lovemaking. Recreation for the labourer, you could say. Still, it's probably wiser to go. I have a pile of letters to answer and you must be getting hot.'

Sheer rage silenced her. She suffered his helping hand when he pulled her to her feet but, as they walked back to the Land Rover, she said in her stiffest voice, 'I wonder if you realise how chauvinistic that observation was. Do you really feel entitled to view me as a little light recreation?'

The sun was blinding in his hair, dazzling in her eyes so that she couldn't see beyond his amusement. 'Don't be stuffy. I have no intention of forcing myself on you, but I can't see why we——'

'I don't go in for casual affairs,' she interrupted brusquely, disappointed, and furious with herself for being so.

'Casual?' A sudden thread of taunting hardness altered the texture of his voice. He was smiling without humour, half closed eyes focused on her mouth. 'My heart, your response may be casual, I can assure you mine isn't. It's a long time since I've felt quite so intense about anything. Like you, I don't view desire through romance's rosy haze, so you needn't worry about breaking my heart. It's pleasant to find a woman with a masculine attitude to such things. Unusual, too.'

'Oh, my God!' She flung up her hands. 'The ultimate male accolade!'

He was laughing openly at her, the harsh strength of his features softened by amusement which was genuine. He had, she realised ruefully, been teasing her.

'You,' she said, promising retribution, 'are a devil! I'll bet no little girl was safe when you were a boy.'

'Ask Phil, she and I grew up together.'

Which might explain the housekeeper's watchfulness. Perhaps she felt possessive about Blake.

If so, it was probably the only form of possessiveness he would allow. He was very much his own man, like her except that his confident independence was tinged with nothing like her own wary regret. He was quite satisfied with his life.

Somewhere she had read that a cynic was a bruised romantic. The break-up of her parents' marriage had caused her attitude towards commitment; her engagement had reinforced the necessity for caution. Her fiancé had not been the only one hurt. Perhaps Blake's marriage had hardened him. As they packed up and drove back, Finley stole a swift glance at the clear, rugged profile and shivered, because a woman who fell in love with him would be asking for trouble. He made conditions, set his own limits, and although he was the most compelling man she had ever met, she recognised that beneath the teasing charismatic surface there was pure steel all the way through.

The rest of the day passed quietly. After settling Finley in a wide hammock beneath a pohutukawa tree, Blake disappeared into his office. A little later, clearly obeying instructions, Phil arrived with a large jug of lime juice and ice cubes and set it on a table within reach, smiling aloofly at Finley's instinctive protest.

That smile irritated Finley, as did the magazines which Phil produced, big glossy things almost filled with photographs of anorexic models in ugly clothes, she decided sourly.

'Blake said that my clothes were on their way across,' she said, 'Have they arrived?'

'Yes, but I'm afraid I haven't had time to unpack them yet.'

And damn you too, Finley thought, climbing out of the hammock in the usual undignified way. Well, a total lack of poise and grace wasn't going to sink her any further in the older woman's eyes, she seemed to be already as far down as she could go.

'You don't need to unpack for me,' she said with her sweetest smile, the one which warned those who knew her best that she was perilously close to losing control of her temper. 'If you'd like to show me my room I'll do it myself.'

The housekeeper's lashes flickered, but no emotion showed in her face as she said, 'Of course,' and led the way back to the house.

Finley had already seen the entrance hall, a luxurious fantasy of mellow old parquet half-hidden by even more mellow Oriental rugs, with exquisite floral trails hand-painted on the walls and a chandelier of an opulence Finley found as mind-blowing as the magnificent Venetian mirror and console beneath it. But it was the suspended staircase which dominated the hall, a miracle of grace and strength and lightness. Phil had every right to that faint air of propietory pride, for everything in the house bore the patina of loving care.

And that included the bedroom she showed Finley into, an enormous pale peach room with a four-poster bed draped in a more intense shade of the same colour and another exquisite mirror, Adam-style this time, above a French desk. A gilt chandelier illuminated a white marble fireplace, a splendid chaise-longue and two armchairs. There were flowers and a bookcase, a bureau and a lovely dressing-table.

The only thing which looked at all incongruous was Finley's suitcase.

'The bathroom is through that door,' Phil told her, indicating a door in the far wall.

'What is through the other door?'

Perhaps the housekeeper had not heard her. She certainly made no attempt to answer. Finley hesitated, then went across to the other door and opened it. And there was what was obviously Blake's bedroom, the pair to hers, decorated with the dark, smooth luxury of superb modern Italian furniture.

After one all-encompassing glance Finley closed the door. She stood looking down at her fingers on the door handle, noting that they were trembling. Almost immediately she lifted her head and smiled at the waiting housekeeper.

'You know, I'd love to be able to see the sea from my room, if it's at all possible,' she said, astounded at how even and pleasant her voice sounded. 'Would it be too much trouble to change?'

Something altered, eased, in the other woman's expression. 'No, it would be no trouble at all. There's a very pretty room just along the corridor.'

It *was* very pretty, not so big as that other room but just as beautifully furnished, this time with a charming Victorian brass bed covered in white lace; the rest of the room was decorated in soothing almond green and white. It did not open on to the wide pillared gallery but, from the long window, the sea beckoned through a screen of trees.

'Lovely,' Finley said politely. 'I'll unpack now. What time is lunch?'

'Midday.' Phil Allen gave a sudden, beguiling grin. 'Dawn starts are the rule here, so we eat early. I'll bring you breakfast at half-past eight, as Blake has had his and is gone by eight. Dinner is at seven-thirty and everyone's usually in bed by eleven.'

'I can come down to breakfast,' Finley told her firmly, 'I'm used to getting up early, but thank you, it was a nice thought.'

Apparently she had passed some kind of test, although the housekeeper still hadn't opened up entirely. As Finley unpacked her clothes she wondered just whose idea it had been to put her in that so accessible room next to Blake's. If it was the housekeeper's she had a damned nerve. Somehow, she rather hoped that it hadn't been Blake's. It was stupid, and dangerously vulnerable of her, but she didn't want him to be capable of such crassness.

Her clothes stored in a handsome kauri wardrobe which would have dwarfed any modern room, she showered in the miniscule golden bathroom, eyeing a selection of expensive toiletries before using her own. By now she was exceedingly thoughtful. She was not used to such luxury. Blake Caird was not just rich, he was excessively, inordinately, possibly fabulously so. She knew little about antiques, but it did not need a connoisseur's experience to tell her that almost everything in the house was a collector's piece. Just how much cold, hard cash the furniture alone represented she had no idea, but she was prepared to believe that it was more than she was likely to earn in a well salaried lifetime.

And that was just the furniture. Her gaze drifted thoughtfully from a superb watercolour on the wall to an exquisite Chelsea bowl which held pot-pourri on a bureau. Until now, she had thought that such wealth only existed overseas; it was a shock to realise that there were people in New Zealand who lived in such beauty and opulence.

Not that it would make any difference to her feelings. She had no intention of becoming his mistress. That decision had been made in sheer self-defence; Blake was far too dangerous for her to cut her teeth on. But she couldn't stop herself from wondering, with a shaming pang of jealousy, just how many women had waited in that beautiful bedroom for him to open the connecting door.

The healthy anger kept her head high as she walked unseen through the house to the side door where the spaniel waited, not exactly agitated, but obviously pleased to see her.

'Come on, silly old thing,' she said affectionately, and smiled as he followed her back to the hammock. She had bought a selection of paperbacks she had intended to catch up on, but she was not able to concentrate. Within a few minutes her lashes drooped and she slept.

It was the dog's growl which woke her. That, and the unnerving sensation of swooping through the air.

'What——?' she demanded foggily, as her body curved automatically to accommodate the hard contours of the one she rested against.

'Go back to sleep,' Blake commanded.

She could hear his smile in his voice and dragged her reluctant eyes open, saying with dignity spoilt by a yawn, 'I can walk, put me down . . .'

'Can you?' He set her on her feet, quelling Blackie's rumblings with a word.

In spite of her brave words Finley sagged. Another yawn split her face; she leaned into him, grateful for the strength which kept her upright. It was sinfully pleasant to be dependent, to feel his hard male power supporting her. And then certain unmistakable stirrings in her body warned her of her vulnerability and she straightened.

'Oh dear,' she yawned. 'I wonder why I always feel so ghastly after a sleep in the daytime.'

'Biorhythms?' He grinned and bent to kiss her nose, holding her small frame protectively in his arms.

The temptation to give in to such cosseting almost overwhelmed her. Almost. With a wry little smile she pulled free, running a hand through the tangled silk of her hair as she faked another yawn. 'Quite possibly biorhythms,' she returned lightly.

'I hoped I might get you up to your room without waking you.' He draped his arm over her shoulder, guiding her back to the house. 'You were sleeping like the dead but the sun was about to reach your face.'

'One thing people in my line learn very early on is to wake quickly. I'll just go up and wash my face and do something to this hair.'

His fingers moved slowly through the heavy swathe of it, stroking gently behind her ear in a sensuous little caress. He stopped, turning her into her arms, a smile tugging at the controlled line of his mouth as he said softly, 'Your eyes are green—the purest, clearest green, exactly the colour of the lagoon around the coral atoll. You're not precisely beautiful, little doctor, but when I close my eyes I can see your face smiling at me, and I want you to smile only for me.'

'You must have a lot of Irish blood,' she retorted breathlessly. 'Did your grandfather kiss the Blarney Stone?'

'Never asked my grandmother.' Devilment and sensual appraisal lit the depths of those strange eyes. 'Caird is Scots Gaelic, so perhaps there was a touch of Irish a long time ago. The Celtic strain is prone to melancholy, but as there is Norse and some good English yeoman stock to anchor the bloodline, I think we can discount too much romantic fervour from the Celt.'

His mouth came closer, offering the sweets of paradise, the torments of hell. Transfixed, Finley closed her eyes and surrendered, opening her mouth to the exploration of his.

It happened just as it had before, the incandescent flare of sensation overpowering the cool, rational processes of the brain, the triumph of the flesh over intelligence. They kissed as if they had exchanged souls and were to be parted for ever, as if life held nothing more for them but this striving for a union so complete that they could never again be separated.

The sun blazed orange through Finley's closed eyelids, its heat blending with the other more powerful heat deep within her. She moaned deep in her throat, her hands sliding across his back to lever herself closer into the magical aura of his sexuality. She was burned by the heat radiating from him but she could not escape; her hips began to move in a rotation as old as time.

His big body tensed. He muttered something, his voice so thick she could not understand the words, before his arms tightened and she was lifted so that he could bury his face in the softness of her breasts. Some hitherto inviolate part of her psyche melted. The harsh compulsion of passion was as tangible as the bite of his arms around her small slenderness. For long moments while he held her clamped to his straining body, she felt an anticipation so violent that she forgot everything but her need.

'I don't understand this,' she whispered through bitten lips. 'Blake, you frighten me.'

He lifted his head. Slowly the blind, impersonal passion which tightened his features was replaced by sardonic weariness.

'It's known as sex,' he said finally as he put her back on to the ground. He could not banish so quickly the physical evidence of his arousal; like her, his skin was flushed across the cheekbones and there was a taut, waiting quality to his stance. But his voice was bored, and his lashes hid eyes which lacked the golden glitter she had seen whenever they rested on her.

The dog gave a plaintive little yelp then sat down, watching them with his head tipped to one side.

'I know *that*.' Finley swayed slightly as she bent to rub Blackie's curly head.

'So, what don't you understand?'

She reacted to the hint of insolence in his tone by standing up straight, her small chin defiantly squared as she glowered at him.

'I don't understand,' she bit out, 'why I should feel like—well, the way I do when I don't think I like you very much.'

The bored irritation vanished to be replaced by the smile she secretly found irresistible. 'Liar. You like me very much.'

'I don't *know* you.'

'What on earth has that to do with anything?'

Chagrined by his scorn, she said in a goaded voice, 'I think it should have a lot to do with it! I told you before, I don't indulge in casual affairs.'

'How about a serious one?'

He was laughing at her and she reacted with much less discretion than normal. 'Not *any* affairs, Blake,' she snapped.

There was the strangest little silence. His expression didn't change, yet she knew that behind the tough unyielding features his brain was working with speed and precision to reach the only conclusion. She did not regret her virginity, but she was grateful that he showed no surprise.

'Wait a minute,' he said, catching her elbow to prevent her from turning away. 'No affairs, Finley? Not ever?'

If he had sounded more than mildly interested she would never have found the grit to answer. As it was, her face was flushed and she could not look at him. 'Not ever,' she said flatly. 'No affairs, no one-night stands. Nothing.'

His fingers slid from the vulnerable inner angle of her elbow to encircle her wrist. Against her skin they were very strong, very dark; the contrast was almost barbaric in intensity.

'Any particular reason? I know it's not a general disinclination.'

His deliberate evocation of the embraces they had shared made her blush even more fiery. She had revealed far more than she intended and she was damned if she was going to defend a very private decision. So she shrugged and said, 'Why not?'

His fingers tightened momentarily and then she was free. In a voice which accepted that he had no right to probe further he said, 'We'd better have lunch before Phil starts shouting.'

She doubted that he cared much about Phil's feelings; she was prepared to swear that no one had any influence on his actions at all, but she went with him. The dog crouched beneath her chair as she enjoyed iced avocado soup, followed by chicken pieces cooked in an oriental sauce of green ginger, honey, soy sauce and sesame seeds. With the meat, Phil served orange and onion salad tabbouleh, a delicious Lebanese concoction of cracked wheat and tomatoes and herbs which was a favourite of Finley's. She ate with delicate hunger, responding politely to Blake's polite and intelligent dissection of a newly published novel, and his hard-edged comments on the latest news.

He was, she realised afresh, a very clever man, and felt ashamed because she had to overcome a certain astonishment at this. It was still hard for her to reconcile the sheer physical power she had watched him display as he replaced the fence-post, with the urbane man who lived in such sophisticated style, like the monarch of a thriving kingdom.

Which only showed that she was not immune from succumbing to stereotypes! Her eyes drifted from the exquisitely set table to the far wall which was graced by a Gainsborough, or a very good copy. Thoughtfully, her gaze returned to her host's face. There was a definite resemblance, although the eighteenth-century subject of the painting had been a handsome man, and Blake was not.

But he had presence. And he acted on her like a potent aphrodisiac. Her eyes dropped to her plate. It was a moment before she managed to put enough starch in her voice to make some innocuous comment about the house.

'When my grandfather bought the place it was decorated in tartan,' he said, and laughed at her undisguised horror. 'He liked it like that, so it wasn't until the fifties that it was redecorated, with a total lack of distinction. About ten years ago, an aunt of mine decided to do something about it. She found a lot of good stuff in the attics but I swear she drove every antique dealer here and in the UK crazy before she was satisfied.'

'She did a brilliant job.'

'She's a brilliant woman. She cut her teeth on Hunter's Valley, the homestead she owned with her husband. It's a superb evocation of a Georgian house. At the moment she's having a marvellous time renovating a Victorian villa not far from here, across the channel.' He grinned at some private joke and leaned back in his chair, surveying her from beneath the sweep of those lashes. 'You'll like her. She scares the hell out of me, she is the toughest woman I know, almost totally without sentiment, but her son adores her and, much to everyone's relief and surprise, so does his wife.'

'Is that Clary Caird?'

'Yes.' He smiled again, affectionately, and she was suddenly bitterly envious of the woman who could bring that look to his face. 'My cousin is a lucky man. You met him, didn't you?'

'Both of them,' she said cheerfully, determined to keep things light. 'It was not, however, exactly a social occasion.'

He chuckled at that. 'No. Morgan said it was quite the most shattering experience of his life and that Clary is not ever going through that again.'

'He'll get over it,' Finley said drily. Without warning, one of the waves of weariness which were part of the aftermath of pneumonia submerged her. Little beads of sweat sprang out across her upper lip and temples. She must have gone grey because he was at her side before she had time to move, his voice sharp and concerned as he asked her what the matter was.

'Sorry. I'm still a bit wobbly. I'll be fine in a—Blake!'

He had scooped her from her chair as easily as if she were a child and was headed for the door.

'Do you have a thing about carrying women around?' she protested. 'It will be over in a moment.'

His voice rumbled in his chest. 'I like carrying you. Don't deprive me of a chance to feel protective. These days women are so capable, it's a rare man who gets an opportunity to indulge his desire to be strong and powerful.'

'I'm sure.' Her sarcasm was comfortable, barely there. He was stronger than most and he knew it, just as she knew that he didn't need such pampering of the ego. Drowsily, enjoying the sensation of being cared for, she said, 'I didn't want to be a nuisance.'

She felt his chest lift but his laughter was not audible and when she looked up it seemed to have been directed at himself. There was almost a derisory twist to his lips as he answered.

'I have this strange premonition that you are going to be a danger out of all proportion to your size.'

'Dangerous? Me?' She lifted her heavy eyelids and gave him a slow smile, unaware of the slumbrous promise in it. Wistfully she said, 'I wish I was. I've always fancied life as a *femme fatale*. I suppose it would have its uncomfortable moments, but you'd never be bored!'

'Are you often bored?'

'Don't have time to be.' Her smile was lazy, sleepy. 'No, life as a house surgeon is guaranteed to banish boredom. I'm always tired, frequently exhausted, invariably busy, so boredom hasn't a chance. Anyway, a *femme fatale* would be wasted as a pediatrician.'

'You might have to do violence to your principles,' he said, as he opened the door to her bedroom. 'My experience of shady ladies is strictly limited, but I would imagine that virginity would be one of the first things to go, if you were serious about your vocation.'

Ignoring the lace cover, he deposited her on the bed and straightened up, watching with amused eyes the blush which his last comment had produced.

For once, Finley hadn't a word to say. Transfixed by the strange, teasing tenderness in his eyes she lay like a doll on the lace, unaware of the dog's quiet snuffling as he turned around several times at the foot of the bed before settling into sleep.

'Go to sleep,' Blake said, and bent and kissed her lightly on the forehead.

CHAPTER FOUR

PNEUMONIA, she decided when she woke, certainly had a debilitating effect on the system. All this sleeping! Yawning, she padded across the wide, polished boards to the window, to watch with dreamy, satisfied eyes the wavelets which ebbed and flowed in ephemeral little flurries on the gold-white sand.

From somewhere close by children's voices rose, pure and high into the air. Finley smiled, craning to see where they were. After a moment she caught sight of them, two small boys of about six solemnly popping the buds on a fuchsia bush. An ache tightened her throat. She liked children immensely, and the cultivation of professional detachment had been difficult for her, a process she was not sure she would ever complete.

But these boys were not ill, not submitting with uncomprehending trust to examinations and drugs and pain. They were vital and totally absorbed in what was possibly a forbidden pleasure. Sure enough Phil's voice, half amused, half admonitory, jerked both heads around.

'Out!' she commanded, unseen by Finley. 'You know you're not allowed here. Mr Caird has a visitor and she's asleep up in one of the bedrooms right now! Come away before you wake her up.'

Obediently they ran across the lawn to where she stood at the side of the house, one asking, 'Why is she asleep in the daytime? Is she a baby?'

Their laughter contained the clear unfettered enjoyment of happy children. Behind the glass Finley smiled, too.

'No, she's been sick.' Phil's voice was stern. 'Off you go, now.'

'Can we have a goodie?'

'*May* we have a goodie.'

More laughter before they disappeared and their voices died away. Finley chuckled and opened the wardrobe, flicked through the clothes there and finally pulled out a terracotta dress.

Downstairs, she followed her instincts until she arrived at the kitchen, an enormous, superbly equipped room big enough to cater for a ball. The two boys were ensconced at a table devouring orange juice and biscuits, and chattering non-stop to Phil as she kneaded bread.

Finley's arrival brought an abrupt silence and from the housekeeper a questioning lift of the brows, but she responded pleasantly to Finley's greeting, even introducing the boys without more than a pause to mark her hesitation. They were Jason and Mark, and they viewed this strange guest of Mr Caird's with unabashed curiosity.

'What can I get you?' Phil asked.

'You're busy,' Finley said. 'I'd love a glass of orange juice, but let me get it.'

The housekeeper looked down at her doughy hands. 'There's a jug of it in the fridge. The glasses are in the cupboard—Jason, show Miss MacMillan where I keep the glasses.'

Jason leapt to his feet and showed her, then stood eyeing her as if he expected to see her collapse any moment. 'Are you sick?' he asked.

'I was, but I'm getting better.'

That satisfied them both. Mark volunteered, 'Jason's got a baby sister. She sleeps in the daytime too.'

'Babies sleep a lot, don't they?' Finley drank some of the juice and grinned at them. She could feel Phil's attention and wondered why the housekeeper was so unwilling to accept her, but there was no need to wonder how the boys felt. She knew how to deal with children. A few minutes sufficed to make them sworn friends, the boys' tongues tripping as they regaled her with stories of school, their prowess at swimming and fighting, and the enormous kite Mark's big brother was making in the holidays when he came home from boarding school.

They laughed a lot, answered questions and asked more, made a fuss of a rather timid Blackie, and thoroughly enjoyed themselves until Phil broke the session up by suggesting a couple of mothers might be starting to wonder where their sons were.

Then Finley washed glasses and plates, while Phil put the bread in to rise.

'You mustn't let them become pests,' Phil said. 'They can be a bit of a nuisance. They tend to follow newcomers about.'

'No matter. I like most children.'

'You've certainly got a way with them. Young Mark's usually so shy you can't get a peep out of him.'

Finley smiled. 'A part of my job is coaxing children to talk. It's a knack, like any other. Do all the children go away when they get to high-school age?'

'Yes, the school is only primary, of course. Most board in Auckland and come home each weekend. It means you lose them when they're twelve.'

'I suppose that's one of the disadvantages of living in Paradise,' Finley retorted lightly, well aware that she had been warned, and amused by it. The older woman must consider Blake totally irresistible if she thought that after knowing him for little more than twenty-four hours Finley was contemplating marriage!

'One of them.'

Finley decided to make her position clear. 'Don't tell me any others. I shall only be here for a few weeks and when I'm back in Auckland and this seems like a dream, I want it to be a perfect one. So, no snakes in Eden, please! Is there anything else I can do?'

'No, thank you, you shouldn't be doing that.'

'Oh, do you like your kitchen to yourself? Sorry.'

Phil shot her a swift, considering look before giving a sudden grin. 'Yes, I do like my kitchen to myself, so that no one can see the awful things that happen in it.'

'Like beating lumpy white sauce with the egg-beater?'

'Every time. And curdling the mayonnaise. But potatoes are the worst. I have great difficulty in getting potatoes cooked without singeing them.'

Friendly relations more or less established, they smiled at each other. Blackie whined and butted at Finley's foot with his nose. 'Do you think he wants something?' she asked anxiously. 'Perhaps he wants to go for a walk?'

'I'd wait until he puts a bit of condition on,' Phil advised. 'He needs food, not exercise.'

'Well, we'll go and find a chair and look forward to dinner,' Finley said cheerfully. 'You are a superb cook, Mrs Allen.'

'Oh, call me Phil, everyone does. And if you want to convince me that you meant that compliment you had better eat a little more than you did at lunch.'

'There's not a great lot of me to keep fed.'

'You're a tiny thing but you're too thin, even so. See that you do better at dinner. Blake should be ready by six-thirty or so. He's usually in by then.'

'What should I wear?'

'What you have on will be fine, he doesn't go in for much formality.'

Finley nodded. Her dress was a timeless classic but, for dinner, she would put on high heels and some make-up. 'I have letters to write,' she said. 'I think I'll do them in that little summer-house I can see from my bedroom window.'

So she wrote to her father, telling him of her adoption by Blackie. He would find that amusing, something to tell his other family. While bees plundered the nectar and pollen from the stately lilies which surrounded the little building, she wrote a few lines on a postcard for the couple who lived in the flat next to hers, made an amusing story of the situation for her godmother in

Canada, and finished with another shot in a seemingly never-ending war she was having with the computer of a department store where she was foolish enough to have an account. It was billing her for a water-bed which she had never seen, let alone purchased.

When she had finished she sat for a moment, hands clasped on the table, and looked about her. Normally, she found late afternoon a sad time of day, at least until the sun went down, but Motuaroha possessed something different in the way of atmosphere. Instead of that stale, tired feeling there was a sensuous warmth about the day, a kind of golden enchantment which rendered the afternoon as expectant and eager as the morning.

Muted by distance she heard voices and the clop of horses' hooves along the road. In one of the houses someone was practising the piano, playing arpeggios with verve and skill. Gulls called as they soared over the beach and, not very far away, a thrush, its spendid buff chest patterned in speckles, hopped gingerly over a small patch of earth. The sounds of the waves and the bees blended with a tentative breeze; even as Finley listened it died away in the still beauty of evening. Blackie sighed, and moved his head to settle it more comfortably on her sandalled feet.

Strangely, Finley felt a sudden rush of moisture to her eyes. She was not normally prone to tears so it had to be part of the lingering weakness left by her illness. She sat very still, grasping at every sensory detail, trying almost desperately to imprint it on her brain, so that when the winter came and she had left Motuaroha far behind she would be able to take the memory out and be transported back through time and space to this day, this moment.

A bitter little quirk of the brain had her trying to imagine the face of Blake's wife, the beautiful red-headed woman who had felt imprisoned by the island. What room had she been locked in before that hysterical dash to freedom and death? Was it that enormous, opulent room with its austere luxury where Blake slept, or had he changed to another room after her death?

Slowly, not unwillingly, her head turned so that she could see along the wide gallery which ran the length of the house. No, she decided, he would not have changed rooms. There had been no sign of love in that harsh face when he spoke of his wife, just a kind of bitter regret so heavily flavoured with cynicism that Finley had been shocked.

Her eyes searched the façade, found the windows that had to belong to his room. They were open and, as her vision adjusted to the shadows behind the pillars, Finley realised that she was under surveillance from within. He was barely visible except for the wheat-blond flame of his hair but after a second or two she made out his outline, enlarged by dimness, almost threatening.

Her skin prickled, every tiny invisible hair pulled vertical. She couldn't move, not to breathe, not to lift her hand in the casual wave which was probably what he expected. Blackie stirred and gave a funny growling whimper, his head lifting as he sensed her unease. It was like being caught in some time-warp, held unwillingly in stasis while all about her the late afternoon drowsiness began to quicken into the renewed vigour of dusk.

Then he was gone, as though he had never stood there, and her lungs hurt with the effort of drawing breath. Clumsily, shaken and unnerved by her reaction, Finley got to her feet, huddled her letters together and set off towards the house, intent on getting up to her room before he emerged from his, so that she could have a breathing-space.

She didn't make it. When she came in through the door he was half-way down the stairs, almost overwhelming in an Italian silk shirt above trousers which moulded his powerful thighs with altogether too much fidelity for any woman's peace of mind. He had far too much style to wear skin-tight clothes, he didn't go in for the obvious, but what he wore was superbly tailored to make the most of his masculine assets.

'If you leave the letters on that tray,' he said, 'they'll catch the ferry tomorrow morning.'

'Thank you.' Her mouth was dry; it was all she could do to articulate the words.

Depositing the letters gave her a chance to move away from him. He stood at the bottom of the stairs, his eyes watchful beneath the thick screen of his lashes, a curious half-smile not softening in the least the line of his mouth.

'You look charming,' he said softly, when she had no further excuse to stay on the other side of the hall.

Startled, Finley met the lazy appreciation in his amber gaze. 'So do you,' she said drily, realising with alarm that her mouth was drying again. 'I'll just go up and put some make-up on.'

'No need.' He slid a hand under her elbow, causing little pulses of pleasure to throb all through her body. 'Come and have a drink.'

For a moment she resisted but, with a tiny shrug, gave in and let him lead her to a room which had a widely striped tent ceiling, white cane furniture and interesting plants. Windows and doors opened on to the brick terrace; clematis and another climber with scarlet trumpet flowers clung to the pergola which shaded the room from the worst of the afternoon sun.

'What would you like?' he asked, settling her into a chair cushioned in blue.

'Fruit juice, please.' At his lifted brow, she gestured at herself. 'My limit is two glasses of wine with food and a liqueur afterwards. Any more than that and I'm definitely not responsible for anything I might say or do.'

'Sensible woman,' he said, adding regretfully, 'although I'd like to see the effects of three glasses of wine. Try this.'

Finley eyed the pink mixture with some apprehension but a tentative sip reassured her. The blend of fruit juices was just as she liked it, slightly acid and very refreshing.

Blake drank whisky, well-watered, and set out to entertain her. He was a marvellous host, a laconic, thoughtful speaker, and they discovered that they shared plenty of interests, from Handel to hydroponics and the best way to cope with rust in cars. From there they proceeded to an appraisal of the country's future; Blake was giving her a crisp run-down of the options open to primary producers when Phil appeared.

'Sorry, Blake it's Mr Oxten on the phone.'

He excused himself, and reappeared within a few minutes, brows drawn together. 'That was a friend of mine. He wants to bring a party up from Auckland on his yacht.'

Finley felt awkward. 'I'll go back to the hotel,' she said.

'Don't be an idiot.' He sat beside her, still frowning, and took her hand in his, his thumb absently moving across the fragile wrist. His expression was enigmatic. 'If they find you in residence I'm afraid the usual assumption will be made. I don't spend all my time alone.'

Well, no. Naturally. A man as vital, as masculine as he was would not need to go far for enthusiastic lovers. Finley realised that if it weren't that she was too level-headed and sensible to indulge in fruitless emotions, she might have to admit that she was being attacked by jealousy.

Her chin lifted fractionally. She met his bland gaze with as much worldly composure as she could manage. 'So, what is there to worry about?'

'What indeed?' he said lightly. 'I think I felt a protective urge, but clearly it was unnecessary. It can only rebound to my credit if you are taken for my mistress.'

The knowledgeable note in the deep voice made her wince, but she shook her head and smiled with irony.

'Oh, I'm sure I'll be in good company,' she said, matching his cynicism.

'Modesty and discretion forbid an answer to that.'

Finley's hand twisted. He released her, but not before raising her wrist to his lips, his eyes gleaming with predatory satisfaction at her instinctive response.

In spite of Phil's superb dinner the evening was spoiled for Finley. Blake seemed to retreat into a bored sophistication laced with something which came close to patronage. It set Finley's teeth on edge, but she endured it without visible reaction. She was, in fact, rather touched by the protective urge he had admitted to, and regretful that her independence had prevented her from accepting that protection. It would, however, be all too easy for a woman to grow dependent on his strength and authority. And, although she might look only eighteen, she was capable of looking after herself.

And too mature, she thought savagely, after parrying another smoothly acerbic comment, to indulge in tantrums just because someone failed to live up to her expectations.

Even as she thought it she knew she was wrong. He was not having a tantrum. Somehow she had flicked him on the raw; he was hiding his emotions with that arrogant attitude. Behind his splendid mask there was vulnerability of a sort.

'Am I boring you?' he asked politely.

She gave him a slow, completely charming smile, not attempting to hide the mockery in it. 'Not at all,' she said sweetly. 'It's an education to see how you take a rebuff.'

The amber in his eyes flamed suddenly to gold. Then, as the anger faded to respect, he smiled ruefully. 'You are probably very good for me. I'm sorry I've been so ungracious.'

She should have left it at that. What did it matter what he thought of her? But she found herself strangely eager to explain. 'I was ungracious too. I do get tired of people—not just men, either—who think that because I'm small I'm only half there! I am quite capable of making it clear that I am not your mistress.'

'I believe you, although I'm afraid my reputation may make the task more difficult. I plead guilty to judging you by your size. In mitigation, I can only say that I was brought up to believe that women need care and guidance because they are the weaker sex.'

Finley responded to the wicked teasing thread in his beautiful voice with an even more wicked smile. 'Weaker in which aspects? Mentally? Stamina? Ability to bear pain?'

He laughed, acknowledging her thrust into the heart of the matter, and pulled her with effortless, inexorable ease on to his lap. 'None of those,' he said softly as his hand slid the length of her throat to tilt her chin. 'At this moment, sheer brute strength is what counts.'

'Sheer brute strength is *only* where it counts,' she retorted.

She expected him to kiss her. She even closed her eyes in anticipation. But, apart from the heady thunder of his heart-beat against her shoulder, nothing happened and she opened them again, squinting slightly to bring his face into focus. He was staring at her mouth as though mesmerised by its soft curves, intent, fascinated. Finley's mouth was parched. Unconsciously, she touched the tip of her tongue to the centre of her upper lip, and trembled at the blaze of desire this elicited. A raw, elemental passion fused them together. Finley tensed, felt the answering rigidity of every muscle in the big body which cradled her, and then he closed his eyes, and it was as if a shutter had dropped. When his lashes lifted they revealed a flat gaze, totally lacking in emotion.

Chilled by the immense self-control needed for such a complete withdrawal, Finley said deliberately, 'Anyway, I'd have thought that you'd know too well what it's like to be typecast by size.'

He laughed softly, cynically, and set her on her feet, moving away to select a record and put it on the turntable of the superb set of equipment he had. As the first golden notes of Placido Domingo's voice ravished the ears, he said calmly, 'Oh, indeed I do. It can come in useful. I look like a prize-fighter and I'm a farmer—I can appear quite stupidly bucolic when the occasion calls for it.'

'I'll bet no one makes the same mistake twice,' she said with feeling, wary of the dangerous tension with which he paced the length of the room to pick up the coffee tray.

'Very rarely,' he replied, in a deceptively pleasant voice. 'Some are so rigidly imprisoned by their misconceptions that it takes a little longer.'

No woman was stupid enough to be taken in by any pretence at bovine stupidity. Feminine instincts were well honed, and it would be a very stupid woman who missed the brilliant aura of masculine competence which surrounded him.

'I love this,' she said, nodding towards the turntable. 'He has the perfect voice for it, doesn't he?'

He accepted the change of subject, and the rest of the evening passed in surprising amicability.

As she prepared for bed Finley pondered on that amicability. Blake was not one of those irritating people who felt that every minute should be taken up by conversation, and no matter if it was banal. The silences as they listened to music had been as comfortable as if they were old friends rather than a man and a woman too aware of each other.

'No howling tonight,' she ordered in her severest voice. Blackie regarded her solemnly with his head between his paws. His stump of a tail swished rapidly back and forth across the small sheepskin Phil had found for him. Finley grinned, patted his head and climbed into the lovely Victorian bed.

She had thought that she might lie awake listening to

the silence but, before she had time to realise it, she was opening her eyes to one of the clear, bright mornings the island seemed to specialise in.

It was early but, for the first time since her illness, Finley felt an uprush of energy, and it was with a sparkle to match the morning that she went down the stairs and out into the golden day. For a second, while he was unaware of her presence, she feasted her eyes on Blake.

He was a kind of amalgam of feminine fantasies, she thought in bemusement, her gaze following the lines of his body as he leaned back in his chair. The sun gleamed lovingly on the crown of his hair, gilded the breadth of his shoulders and the fine hair which covered his corded forearms. A man of his size shouldn't possess that rarest of attributes, grace, yet he was supremely graceful, his perfect health and proportions and radiant sexuality combining to delight and torment the eye.

She made no noise but he realised her presence almost immediately and rose, those bright eyes caressing her small, probably dazzled, face with mocking pleasure.

Uncannily echoing her thoughts of a moment before, he said, 'How rare in a person as small as you to find such perfect proportions! Most people of your height need an extra four inches in the legs, but you are ideal.'

Swift, uncontrolled colour heated her skin. 'I'd like the four inches, just the same. Thank you. I could return the compliment.'

He chuckled and slid the chair beneath her. 'Thank you. I'd give you the inches if I could.'

'Would you?'

'No,' he said promptly. 'I've become used to it, but there are occasions when I wish people didn't find my size quite so intimidating.'

'Then you can thank your fortunate combination of genes for giving you grace as well as height,' she said teasingly, and was astounded when dusky colour touched the high cheekbones.

He hid his momentary confusion by attack. Laughter gleamed in the depths of his eyes as he asked, 'Don't very small women have to be careful when it comes to bearing children? If, for example, you were carrying my child?'

A strange heat melted Finley's bones into liquidity. It was all she could do to flick open her napkin, and her hands trembled so much that she had to clench them beneath the table. At her feet, Blackie crunched on a dog biscuit he must have acquired from Phil; the mundane little sound helped stiffen her backbone enough for her to ignore the peculiar sensations in her body and say composedly, 'Yes, quite possibly. Very small women are at a disadvantage when it comes to the reproduction of the species, which probably explains why there are so few of us about.'

'So if you bore my child it could be dangerous?'

Again there was that overwhelming, drenching sweetness, as if her blood was on fire. 'A hundred years ago, quite possibly,' she returned. 'Nowadays we can cope with that sort of thing.'

'Caesarean,' he said calmly. 'Does the prospect worry you?'

'No.' She risked a glance his way, saw that beneath his lashes his eyes were very keen, very hard, and the smile which touched his mouth was almost angry.

'It's not likely to happen for a while,' she said briskly. 'I haven't yet met a man who is prepared to put up with the sort of wife I'd be.'

'Why?'

She shrugged. 'Because I intend to be a pediatric consultant, which means I have to work as a pediatric registrar for five years, and after that I want to go overseas for experience for a couple of years at least.'

His brows lifted at that. 'It does not,' he said drily, 'sound as if marriage is on your immediate agenda. You have eveything carefully planned.'

'God and exams willing,' she said flippantly.

'And nothing is going to stand in your way? Not a love affair or an inconvenient marriage?'

The orange juice was too sweet. She set the glass back on the table and said with a slight snap, 'Exactly. I've worked like a slave for years, given up things that most women of my age take for granted, because I know what my aim is. I don't want anything to get in the way. Is that so surprising? Would you give up this place for a love affair? Or an inconvenient marriage?'

Something ugly tightened his features.

'Oh, God,' she said helplessly, appalled.

The broad shoulders lifted in a half shrug. Very calmly he said, 'No. I refused to allow an inconvenient wife to pressure me into giving up Motuaroha. She died because of my intransigence. I can understand and admire your determination. I suppose what surprises me is that so much ambition is tied up in so small a package.'

The wry irony of his words made her smile. 'You're hopelessly chauvinistic,' she said rather sadly.

'I'm afraid so.' He held out an imperative hand and after a hesitant moment she put hers in it, watching as her thin fingers were hidden by the dark strength of his.

He lifted it to his mouth, kissing her palm with lazy appreciation, his half-closed lids hiding his emotions. His lips were warm and firm. His potent masculinity summoned all that was female in her. Her fingers trembled and she bit her lip as little tremors of sensation began to ripple along her nerves.

'I'd like to change your mind about that love affair,' he said audaciously, a deep current of sensuality warming his tones.

Finley sent him a straight look, her brows knotted to hide the turmoil in her body. 'I have no intention of cutting my teeth on you,' she said firmly.

'Afraid, my heart?'

She responded to his mockery with a fiery glance. 'Yes,' she said simply. 'I don't need complications in my life, I like it as it is.'

'Why, Finley, you're a coward!'

She grinned. 'Yes. I'm also stubborn. You can't tease me into becoming your lover, or force me, or talk me into it——'

'How about if I woo you?'

The smooth provocation of his voice stroked across her mind like warm velvet, infinitely fascinating, infinitely dangerous. Finley sobered instantly. It seemed she had flung him a challenge. That had to be the biggest error in tactics she could have made; the Cairds of this world thrived on challenges.

Hurriedly she said, 'That was not a dare. I can't afford to get involved with you, Blake.'

'I'm desolated,' he said politely, his eyes laughing slivers of gold in his serious face.

'Don't you believe me? I hadn't put you down as conceited——'

'Of course I believe you. I'm just wondering whether to take any notice——'

'—Arrogant, yes!' She interrupted in her turn, unable to stop herself from being seduced by his wicked amusement. 'Definitely arrogant! You'll just have to accept that I will not be fascinated into an affair with you!'

He grinned with thoroughly evil satisfaction, leaning across the table so that he could drop his voice to a suggestive murmur. 'Even though we both know you could be persuaded?'

Finley's lashes drooped to hide the runaway desire which flowed through her. Reluctantly, and only because she knew it was inevitable, she said, 'Even though we both know I could be persuaded. There, is your ego appeased?'

'For the moment.' He buttered a piece of toast before finishing blandly, 'Of course, I make no promises.'

'Oh!'

But she laughed, her face suddenly very young and mischievous and just as teasing as his. He had loads of charm when he chose to use it, the devil. It would be altogether too easy to forget that as well as that disturbing charm he possessed other, more perilous qualities.

One in particular she recognised because she had it too, the ability to be single-minded to the point of ruthlessness. It would be beyond stupidity to allow herself to be lured by that potent magnetism into an affair which, whether consummated or not, could only succeed in hurting her. She needed all her strength to survive the stresses of her profession; she had none to spare for recovering from ill-advised love affairs.

Something of her thoughts must have shown in her expression, for he said calmly, 'However I can promise that I have enough self-control to stop myself from ravishing you when you're not looking.'

She smiled at that, although his words sent little prickles of excitement through her. The images which surfaced in her mind for a fleeting shameful moment almost made her gasp. Firmly, she banished them back into the murky regions of her subconscious.

'You don't know how much reassurance that gives me,' she said, then wrenched the conversation away from these risky paths by asking, 'What time do your friends arrive?'

'They'll be here for lunch.'

She nodded, nibbled a piece of toast and dropped the crust on to the ground. A loud snap marked its safe arrival in Blackie's gullet.

'For your own sake,' Blake said firmly, 'don't feed him at the table. He'll turn into a damned nuisance, demanding food every time you sit down to a meal.'

'OK,' she said peaceably.

He shot her a suspicious look but said nothing. Finley kept her eyes fixed on the coffee, finally saying with a sigh of pleasure, 'Thank heaven I don't have to live in a world without coffee. Or tea. How many people are arriving, and what will I wear for lunch?'

'Six, and what you have on now will be perfect.' He smiled at her sceptical glance down at the little camisole sun-dress, and drawled, 'You look sexy but sweet. They won't have anything elaborate with them, Sam's yacht isn't exceptionally big. Are you nervous at the prospect of meeting some of my friends?'

She was uneasy at the intonation he gave the words. 'No,' she said, casually throwing the monosyllable away. 'Why should I be?'

'Why, indeed?'

After breakfast he took her with him on a short tour of the complex which made up the working heart of the station, the stockyards and implement sheds and the enormous woolshed with its attendant pens. Finley enjoyed herself very much, revelling in the smells and sounds and sights of agriculture, but she could not forget that last innocent-seeming question. He had asked it almost as though he wanted her to find this meeting with his friends important enough to be nervous about.

By the time they came back to the house it was almost midday, and she had only time to shower and pull back on the sun-dress before a raucous blare from a fog-horn indicated the arrival of the yacht.

CHAPTER FIVE

THE *Hauraki* was a ketch, a white and blue thing of sturdy yet gracious lines. From the jetty, Finley and Blake watched as the lovely yacht was skilfully brought into the bay, at first under sail and then with the help of the engine.

'She's Sam's pride and joy,' Blake commented, watching with a knowledgeable eye as the ketch was eased in to the jetty. 'He's had her out in weather any sensible man would stay ashore in.'

If his expertise in berthing was anything to go by, Sam Oxten was a superlatively skilled sailor, Finley decided. A few minutes later she discovered that he was nice, too, he and his wife Fay, but it was the man beside him who caught the eye, for he was quite the most beautiful man Finley had ever seen.

'But we've met,' Morgan Caird said, smiling at Finley, as his wife handed her wriggling son over to Blake and laughed, holding out her hand.

'How lovely to see you again,' she said, her twinkling eyes alight with mischief. 'And in much more propitious circumstances!'

Just behind, a superbly groomed woman looked Finley up and down with faint contempt. Well, Blake had warned her. Her name was Marie Dwyer, and Finley had only to watch her greet Blake to understand why there was no friendliness for her in those large, dark eyes.

Clary Caird's expression was wry, yet amused, and her gorgeous husband was smiling with a hint of the same irony which often marked his cousin's expression. Not that Marie Dwyer was obvious. In spite of the warmth of the kiss with which she greeted Blake she made no attempt to keep him by her and after that first cool moment she was quite charming to Finley but, as they set off towards the house, Finley was conscious of the other woman's gaze on her, especially when Blake looped a casual arm across her shoulders to help her up a steepish pinch in the road. And although Marie Dwyer talked to the sixth member of their party, a pleasant middle-aged man, she did not have her full attention on him.

'You have a new dog, Blake,' Clary said, stooping to pat Blackie.

'He's not mine.' Blake told them of the situation in a laconic style which failed to hide his enjoyment of the situation. Or perhaps it was the reaction of his guests which produced that deep amused undertone in his voice.

For except for Morgan, who was as poker-faced as his cousin, they all looked incredulous, regarding Blake with the dubious expressions of those who have been fooled by someone's off-beat sense of humour before. They looked at Finley, and then at Blackie, trotting along with his nose six inches from her knee, his tail wagging happily in time with his ears.

Clary laughed, and Finley saw why Morgan had fallen in love with her. 'So Beauty and the Beast stormed the impregnable castle,' she said teasingly, casting a sparkling look at Blake. 'Watch out, Blake, fairy-tales have a habit of coming true!'

'Especially the Cinderella story,' Marie Dwyer said sweetly, her dark glance moving to Finley's face.

Sam Oxten said something, rather too loudly, and there was a flurry of conversation during which Finley saw Clary send an admonitory, half laughing glance at her silent husband. Blake too said nothing and for a moment Finley saw an identical expression on both men's faces. Then Blake's lids came down to hide eyes as clear and cold as quartz. A shiver pulled her skin tight. She looked away straight into Morgan's dispassionate gaze and felt unease feather the length of her spine.

Marie Dwyer was either too stupid to be afraid, or infinitely braver than most people. From the sudden fearful comprehension in her face she had not expected Morgan to take her comment to apply to his wife, which made her stupid. And so not worth fretting over. For the first time in her life, Finley was out of her depth. She did not belong here, not on this enchanted island, not in this little kingdom touched by magic.

For 'magic' read 'money', she thought cynically, knowing that she was wrong. These people were larger than life, the women elegant even in their most informal clothes, the men with the unstressed authority which came of total self-confidence. They spoke well, they shared in-jokes, they knew the ramifications of each other's families, they had attended the same schools. Except for Clary Caird, and she was there because Morgan had fallen in love with her.

Only Finley was an outsider. She was also indulging in a most unusual bout of self-pity.

And she was under scrutiny. Blake was watching her with emotionless eyes, as though she was a problem.

Finley stumbled. The arm across her shoulder tightened and he asked beneath his breath, 'Tired?'

'Just clumsy.'

The speculation was replaced by a glimmer of laughter. His lips quirked and Finley felt that lazy, potent charm reach out and envelop her in its warmth.

'We'll be eating a little later that usual, at one,' he said, 'so why don't you slip upstairs and rest?'

'I think I'd better. I feel a bit wan.'

'You look delicious,' he told her, with a teasing gravity which made her smile.

In the end, she waited until after lunch before slipping up to her room, Blackie at her heels like a shadow. She expected to lie on her bed for an hour or so, but she went to sleep and it was much later that she woke to a soft knock at the door.

'Sorry,' Clary said, looking a little concerned, 'but it's after five and Blake was getting a little edgy, so I said I'd check on you.'

'Come on in.' Finley hid a wide yawn. 'Oh, lord, I'll be glad when I can spend a whole day on my feet.'

'Blake said you've had pneumonia, you poor thing. It must have been a bad attack.'

'Oh, well, I was tired to begin with, and I got up too soon.'

'I can imagine. You doctors are always in a chronic state of exhaustion.' Clary had been a nurse. She sat down in a chair, holding out an encouraging hand to Blackie. 'You chose the perfect place to convalesce in.'

Both women laughed as Blackie stayed put long enough for Clary to administer just one pat before he politely removed himself to a position against Finley's leg.

'Very touching,' Clary said.

Finley looked doubtful. 'I should have taken him home, I suppose.'

'If I know my cousin-by-marriage at all, I shouldn't imagine you had much say in the matter,' Clary told her cheerfully. 'They run to autocracy, these Cairds. Overbearing and high-handed from the cradle. Are you sure he didn't kidnap you?'

Laughing, Finley walked over to the mirror to tidy her hair. 'No, he just made staying here seem the only logical thing to do!'

'Typical Caird behaviour. They are born arrogant. What do you think of the next generation?'

'The pick of the bunch so far,' Finley said promptly. 'I'm proud to have had some small part in his birth. Was he born arrogant too?'

'I have a horrid feeling he was.' Clary smiled. 'He has a very lordly way of demanding sustenance which my mother-in-law says reminds her forcibly of Morgan at the same age.'

Blake had been right, Finley did like Clary. She liked Morgan, too. Later that night, in her best dress, a thin slip of silk the exact green of her eyes, Finley watched Blake with his guests and thought sardonically that she could probably learn to like them all. Except for Marie Dwyer, who was being very patronising. They were nice people, the men hiding their essential toughness with charm and courtesy, the women bright and intelligent and interesting. All of them as far removed from Finley's life as this lovely room was different from a hospital ward.

'That pensive look suits you,' Blake murmured a few seconds later. 'The Pre-Raphaelites would have liked to paint you.'

She smiled, her eyes very deep and mysterious. 'They liked tall, willowy women.'

'Their mistake. Come and tell me what to fill your glass with.'

His hand was imperative, his expression a command, yet that strange communion, that sense of understanding, was there. As Finley got obediently to her feet she caught Marie's gaze and read in it an angry contempt which fired her anger. She leaned her head a moment against Blake's arm in a provocative, intimate little gesture.

'I don't think your Miss Dwyer likes me,' she said serenely. 'Shall I put her out of her misery and tell her that I'm not your lover?'

'Why? She's having a wonderful time imagining the worst. Marie thrives on drama. It seems a shame to put an end to her enjoyment.' The caustic note in his voice intensified as he finished, 'Besides, she wouldn't believe you. She doesn't trust her own sex.'

Finley rounded her eyes at him. 'She considers you irresistible? Or insatiable?'

'She was Lisa's—my wife's—confidante. They should have gone on the stage together, they made a fantastic double act.'

The clean chiselling of his features hardened into a mask as Marie came up to them, charm personified, but unable to hide either her curiosity or her chagrin. She spoke to Finley, but her eyes kept flicking up to Blake as if to judge his reactions.

'Clary has just let slip that you work in a hospital,' she said, smiling with carefully considered graciousness. 'It is a terribly responsible job, surely, with all those medicines and things. You must be terribly clever.'

'Brilliant,' Finley agreed, exposing her small white teeth in return.

The older woman was not used to such directness. She stared at Finley with something like scandalised bewilderment. 'How nice,' she said faintly, before recovering enough to direct an arch smile at Blake. 'It's almost impossible to take her seriously, isn't it? She's such a little thing to be a doctor, like a doll.'

Blake embarked on a long, very comprehensive survey of the seething Finley. He was obviously enjoying it, and by the time he finished not only Finley was restless. 'Not at all like a doll,' he said at last. 'Like a fairy child, dangerous because she looks like the real thing but is out of reach, in a different dimension.'

'Fairies can make the change-over,' Finley said, only half joking, 'but always at the cost of their true selves. They lose their magic, and what's a fairy without magic?'

He nodded, his face expressionless. 'Mortals can live in the land of Faerie but they lose their souls.'

And suddenly neither was joking. Marie broke into the suddenly tense silence by saying stiffly, 'How *whimsical*! Do you two often have conversations about fairies?'

Blake smiled, not very pleasantly. 'Whenever I feel like it.' And make what you like of it, his tone challenged. Marie backed away so fast that Finley had to bite her lip to stop herself from laughing, hastily composing her expression when the other woman addressed her with a return of that odious patronage.

Playfully, she said, 'I hope you realise how incredibly lucky you are to be staying here, Finley. Although Motuaroha is made for parties and gaiety, Blake is something of a hermit. You really are wicked,' with a roguish glance upwards, 'because you owe it to your position to entertain more. I don't suppose you realise it, Finley, but the Cairds are one of our oldest families.'

'Fascinating,' Finley said, dead-pan. She didn't dare look at Blake to see how this blatant piece of snobbery went down, but she could feel his resigned scorn.

'You haven't a drink,' he said smoothly. 'Come with us, Marie, and I'll get you one.'

Dinner was a stunning meal. South Pacific food was served out on the terrace, the centrepiece on the long table some superb snapper caught by Phil's husband that morning. Phil had baked them in coconut cream and festooned a pattern of grilled prawns around them. The meal was arranged Polynesian style on green leaves with the gaudy silk of hibiscus flowers lending the right floral note.

Finley ate as slowly as she could, but even so, her small appetite was satisfied well before any of the others. Making a mental note to ask Phil the recipe for the stuffings she had heaped on the avocados, oysters and caviar and some delicious but secretive ingredient, she tried to hide the fact that she had finished.

'Sure you don't want any more?' Clary eyed her own plate ruefully. 'Isn't Phil a marvellous cook? I shouldn't eat nearly so much but I'm still feeding the baby and I have this enormous appetite! Oh my goodness, this green pepper is stuffed with pork!'

She made such a comical face that Finley laughed. 'You don't like pork?'

'Adore it, but I hoped it might have something

relatively non-fattening in it. Like lettuce.'

Finley gave her a quick professional scrutiny. 'You don't look as though you need to diet.'

'She doesn't.' Morgan slid gracefully into the chair on the other side of his wife, slanting Finley a glance which blended amusement and satire. 'Always on call, doctor? It must go with the territory; Clary can't forget that she's a nurse.'

'Oh, yes I can!' Clary grinned into her husband's face, her adoration and trust so openly expressed that Finley was oppressed with a strange desolation. 'Ever since the baby arrived I've been a perfect fool. He gets a tiny rash and I have to be forcibly restrained from rushing off to the doctor!'

The tough assurance, which was another Caird characteristic, softened into tenderness as Morgan smiled at his wife. 'We live in hopes that he never develops a cough,' he teased.

It was a pleasant evening, if one could ignore Marie Dwyer's baleful sidelong glares. That queer little pang of envy fled from Finley as quickly as it had arrived and she enjoyed herself, although she had to fight a strongly possessive instinct whenever she saw Blake talk to one of the other women. Banishing it, she resumed a conversation with Fay Oxten about the Monet exhibition which was to arrive at the Auckland Art Gallery soon.

Shortly afterwards Blake sat down beside her, his eyes searching her face.

'OK?' he asked softly.

'Don't fuss!'

'Stop me,' he invited, his gaze gleaming with danger.

Finley said, 'I feel fine, Blake.'

He accepted that, but with an expression which said that if he thought she was overdoing it he would not hesitate to pack her off to bed like a weary child. She should have been angry, but an ache at the back of her throat revealed how his consideration affected her.

Damn all protective men! Her independence was too
precious to be weakened by a desire to be cherished.

After that, she tried to withdraw from the intimacy
they seemed to have achieved so quickly. Her smiles did
not reach her eyes; she was careful not to be alone with
him at any time. She even toyed with the idea of going
back to Auckland but Marie was eloquent about the
humidity there and she couldn't summon up the strength
of mind to make the decision.

At midnight, Clary picked up her son from the
bedroom where he had been sleeping and they all walked
back to the yacht beneath a sky of darkest velvet
encrusted with the multi-coloured jewels of the stars. On
the horizon another band of glitter, warmer, less remote,
indicated houses on the Whangaparaoa peninsula.

The faint scent of salt mingled with the perfumes of
the night, flowers, the cool dew, the aroma of grass and
animals. Somewhere up the valley a morepork called, his
forlorn little cry at odds with the small owl's ferocity.
Blackie gave an excited whine but refused to leave his
post at Finley's heels.

Fay remarked on the beauty of the night, adding,
'Perfect for lovers.'

Finley was some distance away, but she could see the
way Marie stiffened at the coy little remark. What a
wearing woman! What had Blake's wife found to like in
her? A kindred soul? Finley wondered, banishing with
mockery the cramp of jealousy in her heart.

After they had seen the others on to the yacht, Blake
and Finley turned back, but Finley felt the impact of the
glare between her shoulder-blades. Poor Marie!

Then the deep shade of the trees swallowed them up
and she relaxed. In companionable silence they made
their way up to the house, a glimmering dream in the
starshine.

'Nightingales,' she said softly. 'There should be
nightingales singing.'

'You're a romantic.'

'I'd defy anyone to be a realist on a night like this.' She indicated the dim beauty of the garden, the house with the dark shapes of the hills behind it and, over all, the brilliant flash of the Milky Way.

'And on winter nights, when the wind screams around the eaves——'

Finley laughed. 'Ah, dramatic!'

'Spring, when it rains for weeks and everything is damp and clammy?'

'Who cares, it's spring, isn't it? You're romantic, too—you admit to loving the place.'

'I do indeed.'

Three words, yet they were stark and uncompromising. Finley heard the implacable note in them and felt an odd little chill.

'I think it's time for me to go in,' she said woodenly. 'Goodnight, Blake. I liked your friends.'

'Even Marie?'

'I felt sorry for her. Love appears to have a debilitating effect on her manners and sense of humour.'

'I doubt if she's capable of honest affection,' he said brutally. 'She'd like to be mistress here, and if she could make me suffer a little for the pain I caused Lisa, well, she'd like that too.'

She didn't want to hear any more, especially not if it was about his wife. Faking a yawn, she turned away.

He laughed, a soft little sound beneath his breath, and stopped her with a hand on her shoulder. 'Goodnight,' he whispered and pulled her into his hard warmth, his angry mouth crushing her protest to nothing.

For a moment she remained rigid, but the swift upwelling of desire softened her into pliability so that she groaned and melted against him, fire into rock.

'Sweet,' he whispered, 'you're so sweet. A sweet little siren . . .'

He kissed her eyelids closed, explored the contours of

her face, the soft lobes of her ears, then returned to take another kiss from her parted lips.

The world began to spin away from beneath Finley's feet. A sudden fierceness clenched her hands across his back; she accepted the sensuous probe of his kiss with an answering ardour, mindlessly offering what had never been offered before, to this man she barely knew. The silk of her dress was no barrier; she felt his arousal, welcomed it with a primitive thrust of her hips, arching her neck to give him access to the soft pulse there and the small, high curve of her breasts.

Helplessly, arching with a desire which increased each time he touched her, she ran her hands the length of his back, tugging at his shirt until she found the smooth, heated skin beneath. Her hands clenched into fists as he brushed back the wide neck of her dress to expose her shoulder.

His mouth on her skin was ecstasy, warm and seeking, trailing across the taut flesh with the sure knowledge of experience, calling into life pleasure sources she had never known existed.

'God!' he whispered harshly.

Finley gasped as he picked her up and strode across the lawn to the summer-house where she had written her letters. The perfume of the lilies dazed her so that she made no protest when he put her on the cushions and came down beside her, one leg pinning hers so that she could not get away.

She didn't want to. His mouth on hers was a dark sorcery, loosing a golden tide of sensation so that she trembled and moaned and turned her head to kiss the gentle, irresistible hand which pushed her dress from her shoulders.

'You're so beautiful.' The words were thick, impeded, and she opened her eyes to see that he was staring down at the pale contours of her body partly concealed by the black silk of her tiny camisole. 'So perfect,' he said unevenly, and bent his pale head and took the nipple into his mouth as though the camisole didn't exist.

Finley's whole body jerked in a spasm of indescribable rapture. The choked little cry she couldn't hold back made him lift his head so that he could see her anguished face.

'That has to be the most erotic sound I've ever heard,' he whispered, before resting his head against her slight breasts. Finley's hand stole down to sift through the crisp warmth of his hair; he turned to kiss her fingers and the friction against her sensitive skin brought another muffled little murmur to her throat. She flexed her legs, stretching to rid them of the intolerable ache which racked her.

His hand slid beneath the waist of her fragile little garment and he turned his attention to her other breast, bringing it to life with the warmth and moisture of his mouth while his hand cupped the one he had already stimulated into unbearable life.

'So tiny,' he said, when he had brought her to a delirium of sensation. 'So small, yet so perfect . . .'

She wrenched the buttons of his shirt free, then pushed the material over the shoulders which were blocking the faint light of the stars. A second later her hands were discovering his torso, appreciating with sensuous enjoyment the contrast of skin like heated silk over muscles taut as steel.

Under her exploring fingers his big frame shuddered. His hands slid beneath her, holding her still as he brought himself above her. He was big enough to smother her, yet he was exquisitely gentle, kissing her throat, the sensitive skin beneath her ears, as she became accustomed to the weight of his body on her. The ache in her body intensified, became a fever of need which ate into her bones. She groaned, signalling surrender, and moved restlessly.

Then his mouth swooped, crushing hers, and with one

powerful thrust he destroyed the dizzying fantasy, charging the dream-like atmosphere with a raw passion which should have terrified her.

She did, indeed, whisper, 'No,' but it was barely audible and she could have wept with frustration when he accepted her decision.

Moving quickly, he lowered himself to lie on his side, pulling her head on to his shoulder as his fingers teased the long damp tendrils of hair at her temples.

When she moved to pull her dress to cover her, he said huskily, 'No, just lie still. At the moment, I don't trust myself and wriggling around like that doesn't help.'

She stayed still and, over the minutes, the bewildering ache of desire slowly subsided into lassitude.

They had been playing with fire and it was his control which had prevented them from being burnt. Shame fired in her skin. 'I'm sorry,' she muttered.

'So am I.' His hand clasped both of hers to his chest so that she both felt and heard the wry words.

'I've never felt like that before,' she confessed, shaken into revealing something which was probably better kept hidden.

'Neither have I.' His voice was even drier than before. 'But an affair is not just sex. It would be easy, and oh, so good, to take you, but you'd regret it when you woke up in my bed tomorrow morning.'

She bit her lip painfully, appalled by an almost over-powering urge to give him what he wanted. It would take so little; his heart still thundered beneath her fingers and it would need only the slightest of movements, a kiss, the lightest stroke of her hand—and she would regret it.

'I'm not geared for an affair,' she said gruffly. 'I can't afford to—to expend so much mental energy.'

He laughed at that, without humour and returned drily, 'Or physical, at the moment. You would be a responsive lover.'

'Don't,' she whispered, shocked anew by the images

which sprang into her brain.

'Sorry.' He waited a while then said heavily, 'We'd better go in.'

As she slipped into the badly crushed silk dress she said, 'I think I should go home.'

'Why? I'm not going to slaver over you at every opportunity, if that's what you're afraid of.'

'I can't imagine you slavering at all,' she said indignantly.

The big house was waiting for them, spendid yet comfortable, a home in spite of its luxury. At the head of the stairs Blake put a hand on Finley's shoulder, turning her to face him.

'Don't go home,' he said easily. 'I enjoy your company.'

'You sound surprised.'

He looked tired suddenly. 'I suppose I am. Respect and liking are not emotions I associate with many women. Perhaps it's because you and I are alike. We know what we want and we're prepared to work for it—and pay the price.'

The chandelier spun dark fire in the tips of her hair as she nodded. The contrast between the man who not very long ago had shuddered with passion against her and the man who stood now watching her was disturbing.

In her room she did not go straight to bed. Instead, after she had put on a nightdress, she switched off the lamp and walked over to the window.

She was frightened. Frightened because she was a traveller in a strange land, the country of the heart, and the hazards were greater than she had ever imagined. Even now the palms of her hands were damp as she remembered the incandescent, irresistible force which had swept her into Blake's arms, and almost into his bed. She had never before felt her body flower into arousal in the grip of a sexuality so powerful that her usual defences were no protection at all.

His scent still haunted her nostrils; she thought wildly that if that was the pheromone which everyone seemed so intrigued by, it was no wonder they were interested. If it was bottled, someone would make a fortune from men who wanted a share of his potency!

Slowly, driven by the aching hunger for union which still held her prisoner, she ran her hands across her body, cupping her breasts as he had, wondering what it was about her that had made him shake with desire. His mouth had been hot and seeking, and oh, he was clever, clever and experienced, for he had known that the friction of the silk against her tender nipples had been an erotic *frisson*.

He was all that any woman would ask for in her first lover. Gentle, unexpectedly tender, with an ardent appreciation of a woman's body which had fuelled her own response into a conflagration. Yet, behind the hunger and the passion, there was control enough for him to accept that she was not ready.

And not a sign of anger; she grimaced, recalling other incidents, confidences from friends. Such control had to be a rarity in the masculine world.

Finley's hands fell to her sides. What would he be like, freed from the constraint of that formidable will? No one had warned her that it was dangerous to wonder about a man, to imagine him caught in an emotion too intense for him to control. She knew that her breath came faster through her lips as she played with fantasies and images, but she did not know that that way lay danger.

Some instinct of self-preservation called a halt. Disgustedly, she said, 'Oh, you fool,' and began to turn towards the bed.

A small movement through the window caught her eye. She froze, her eyes narrowing as they searched the shadows beneath a huge poinciana. All was still. She was just about to give up her vigil when the shadows dissolved, coalescing again to form the shape of a person.

Of a woman. Marie Dwyer.

Sheer fury dictated Finley's actions. Pulling back the curtain, she called down, 'Is something wrong, Miss Dwyer?'

The woman jerked as if she had been struck. Then defiantly the black head lifted and the smooth voice came forth, oddly light on the scented air. 'No, I've just been walking. Goodnight.'

'Goodnight.'

In bed, Finley found that her hands were shaking and she felt sick. She should have had difficulty in sleeping, but as usual, she dropped off almost immediately her head touched the pillow.

CHAPTER SIX

OF COURSE she slept in, not waking until ten o'clock. Blackie was gone from his sheepskin and, through the windows, there came the faint sound of voices and laughter.

'Oh dear,' Finley said guiltily and used all of her expertise to get dressed and downstairs in fifteen minutes, and that included tripping over the dog outside the door and saying good morning to him in due form.

It had been years since she had felt shy, and there was no need for her to be embarrassed, but it took quite an effort to walk out on to the terrace. They greeted her with a little mild teasing about her sleeping habits, teasing which seemed to her to hold an unspoken implication that she had spent the night in Blake's bed. Perhaps she was too sensitive; it didn't help to have to meet Marie's burning gaze every time she looked up.

Still, she smiled and made the expected light rejoinder, met Blake's mocking regard with cool poise and allowed herself to be seated by him and plied with coffee and rock-melon. She spooned passion-fruit pulp over the musky, richly flavoured flesh and ate with dainty, absorbed greed while they talked and teased with the relaxed ease of old friends. In a wicker basket, the Cairds' baby cooed and blinked at his little starfish hands, and smiled an adorable triangular smile at his thoughts and anyone who came within his field of vision, including one curious spaniel.

'Here Blackie!' Blake's command dragged the dog back to his place under Finley's chair.

The baby bellowed, scarlet and furious.

'Oh, that nasty Caird temper,' Clary sighed, swooping to pick him up. 'When you are bigger, darling, you can have a dog of your own, but this one is Finley's. You're a hungry, tired boy, aren't you? Come on, we'll do something about it.'

Morgan went with his wife. A moment later Sam Oxten exclaimed, 'Look at the birds working in the bay!'

The other man said that he could see the fish jump, and there was a general exodus of eager fishermen. Blake looked down at Finley. 'Do you want to come?'

'No, thank you, I'll just sit and watch you. I'm no fisherman.'

'I'll keep you company,' Marie said sweetly.

Blake lifted a brow. As Finley smiled a signal that she could cope, she realised that he must have heard her accost Marie last night.

Protective, she thought drily, her eyes lingering on the broad shoulders and long lithe body. He nodded and followed the others.

There was an ominous silence, broken by Phil's arrival.

'Miss—er—Finley hasn't finished yet,' Marie told her curtly.

Finley stared at her in astonishment, then at Phil, and was relieved to see a serene smile on the housekeeper's face as she continued to stack the dishes on the trolley.

'Can we help?' Finley asked quickly, before Marie could speak again.

'No, you sit there and enjoy the sun. I won't be a moment.'

She wasn't much longer but Marie sat there fuming until she left, and it was in a voice that Phil must have heard that she said, as the housekeeper left, 'If Lisa were still alive she wouldn't dare behave as though she owns the place!'

There was no answer to that. As the outraged words

quivered on the air Finley poured herself another cup of coffee and leaned back in her chair, determined not to be persuaded into a quarrel. She wasn't going to indulge the woman in her spite.

Baulked by her companion's silence Marie said viciously, 'Of course she's in love with Blake. It's a wonder her husband doesn't put a stop to it. Still, he has a nice cushy job here, he'd be a fool to rock the boat.'

Finley's mouth opened, then was firmly closed. When she had regained control she said mildly, 'That could be construed as a slanderous statement. Blake would have every right to object to that sort of gossip.'

Unease, perhaps fear, pulled at Marie's features. 'Well, I didn't mean that there is actually anything between them,' she said edgily. 'Blake could have any woman he wants!'

Such rampant snobbery set Finley's teeth on edge. Her lashes drooped. An unholy wickedness prompted her to murmur dulcetly, 'And presumably does.'

Marie leaned forward, composing her face into earnestness. 'Finley, you should know a little more about the Cairds. Forgive me, but I shouldn't think that you have come into contact with men like them before. They are a breed apart. When men grow up as privileged as *they* are they become arrogant, quite ruthless in their private lives as well as their public, and because they are such magnificent creatures they get away with murder!' She gave an artificial little laugh presumably intended to convey womanly solidarity.

'They?'

'Blake and Morgan.' Of course, her tone implied.

Blinking, Finley objected, 'But Morgan is married. I don't understand——'

'Oh, I don't see that lasting! She's not even pretty. And they don't have anything in common—until Morgan married her no one had ever heard of her!'

She looked smugly across the table, pointing out without words that anyone who mattered would have known of the consternation that Morgan's marriage to a nobody had caused. Finley eased a little further into her chair and settled down to enjoy herself. Such flagrant snobbery was rarely encountered in egalitarian New Zealand and she had every intention of savouring it to the full.

'She comes from the wrong side of the tracks?' she asked.

But Marie caught the amused mockery behind the polite enquiry and snapped, 'Of course not! She's just a nobody.'

She made it sound the ultimate insult; perhaps in her lexicon it was. It was with the complacent certainty of a woman who knows she is lovely that she continued, 'Nobody could understand why he married her. It's not even as though she's a beauty. She's passable, but sophisticated men like the Cairds demand beauty. They're spoilt, of course, they have everything—social position, money, power, and they are incredibly attractive. Beauty is a necessity to keep their interest.' Her mouth twisted, and suddenly she was ugly. 'And even then it often isn't enough. Blake didn't stay faithful to Lisa, and she was the most beautiful creature I've ever seen.'

Astonished revulsion had kept Finley speechless throughout this extraordinary tissue of distortions. She felt befouled. If Marie couldn't see what was patently obvious, that Morgan and Clary were deeply and wholly in love, she was blinded by prejudice. As for Blake's unfaithfulness—Finley rejected the notion completely. Anyone could see that he had too much integrity to indulge in adultery.

Perhaps her face revealed something of her thoughts, for Marie leaned forward again and told her maliciously,

'She had hair the colour of burnished copper and great blue eyes—she looked like a model! Everyone adored her, she was so vivid and bright and sparkling, being with her was like living on champagne. Everything was so much fun when she was there. Blake was completely smitten, he pursued her until he won her, he was so much in love it was astounding. They had the biggest, most important wedding—I was chief bridesmaid.'

And very much in love with the groom! Finley asked, 'So, what went wrong?'

'This place stifled her. Blake said her place was here with him, but Lisa wasn't easily intimidated. They fought—God, how they fought. I think she enjoyed it. She said if she couldn't get to him any other way, at least she could make him lose his temper. But in the end he didn't even do that. He was bored with her, and he left her here alone with his spies while he went on his trips overseas. She hated it.'

Marie spoke smoothly but she directed little sideways glances at Finley, and her pale fingers were held tensely in her lap. How much of this did Marie really believe? Finley was adept at summing people up, and she was inclined to think that Marie saw her as a threat and was trying to frighten her off.

She was speaking again, eagerly, swiftly, assessing Finley's reactions from beneath her lashes. 'She used to ring me and she'd be crying so hard I couldn't understand her. Her parents were no help, they just said that she had known where Blake lived when she married him!'

To Finley it sounded as though Lisa's parents had been only too relieved to get rid of a spoilt hysterical daughter and had no desire to have her wished back on their hands. For which one could hardly blame them.

Poor Blake! And poor Lisa, who should have had the sense to marry a doting, rich city-dweller.

'She was so unhappy,' Marie said softly. 'She had

always been so popular, hundreds of men wanted to marry her, yet after a year Blake refused to sleep with her.'

Sickened, castigating herself for allowing this to go on, Finley got to her feet. Marie gave a little gasp, as though until then she hadn't realised what she had said, yet there was a febrile glitter in the dark eyes which made a liar out of her.

She might have loved Lisa, but she had hated her too, and she had certainly coveted Lisa's husband.

'It's a very sad story,' Finley said in her best professional manner.

'He put her through hell.'

The vindictive tone made Finley shudder. 'I don't suppose either of them were very happy,' she said, surprised to find herself profoundly sorry for this woman who, in a strange way, loved both of the players in the sad domestic drama.

'Happy? My God, would you be happy with a man who refused to make love——?'

'Look, I don't think you should be telling me this.'

Finley fought hard to hide the distaste in her voice, but Marie gave a cynical, tormented laugh.

'Why not, for God's sake, Lisa told everyone who would listen! She quarrelled with him and told him not to expect her to sleep with him until he was prepared to give in, and when she went up to bed that night everything of hers was gone from their room. He had told the housekeeper to clear her things from the main suite. Everything! She wouldn't give in, she thought he'd plead with her to go back, but he never came near her again. I think in the end, she was frightened of him. Nobody had ever rejected her before. He used to look at her as though she wasn't there.'

It sounded as though Blake had married while in the throes of infatuation, and that his wife's immaturity and the tantrums which went with it had driven him away. He was a proud man; Lisa's habit of spreading intimate details of their marriage would have disgusted him further, and her attempted sexual blackmail must have been the final straw.

Finley didn't want to hear about his marriage. She should never have allowed things to go this far. But just as she was about to put an end to it Marie spoke again, and such was her air of desperation that Finley said nothing. Think of her as a patient, she adjured herself sternly, and knew that she was not far wrong. Marie may have begun by trying to frighten her off, but she was unburdening herself now, seeking ease for an emotional load which had grown too heavy for her to carry.

'He was shattered when she died,' Marie said, her voice dragging. 'They'd had another quarrel. She wanted to go to a special party and he refused to take the boat across. It was a wild day, but she said he'd been out in worse weather. Anyway, she said that if he was too afraid to go she wasn't. She'd take the launch. He locked her up in her room. She rang me, she was screaming with temper, she said that that was it, she was leaving him. I tried to persuade her not to do anything foolish, but she wouldn't listen. She climbed out of her window and took the launch. She couldn't handle it, Blake was right, it was far too wild a day to go out and she was almost totally inexperienced. She ran on the rocks at the other end of the island and she was drowned. I heard it on the radio. He didn't ring me . . .'

Tears enlarged her beautiful eyes. She gulped and gave an odd little shiver. In her lap, her thin pampered hands clenched and unclenched.

After a moment she muttered, 'It would take a very special woman to accept that for Blake a wife will always come second to Motuaroha.'

'Yes,' Finley said gently.

With superb timing Clary arrived back, her expression quizzical as she took in the scene before her. Tactfully, she began to tell them of her son's habit of singing as he nursed. Marie followed her lead, refusing to look at Finley as she slid into a dissertation on her nephews, who were, it seemed, the next best thing to paragons.

She was, of course, suffering a certain embarrassment at having revealed so much of herself to a woman she not only disliked but distrusted. Finley hid a wry little smile, and listened as Marie told a remarkably forbearing Clary how to bring up her son.

'Oh, I don't know that I'll be able to do much more than tone down his natural force of character,' Clary said comfortably. 'He's demanding and intent on getting his own way, just like his father. He has, however, a gorgeous smile.'

'Just like his father,' Marie said archly. 'Where *is* Morgan?'

'Out with the fishermen.'

She made a comical face and laughed. Finley liked her very much. She was easy to talk to, with a dry sense of humour which did not hide a basic and very essential kindness. She would have been a good nurse; she would be a good friend. She was certainly very much in love with her handsome husband, and he with her. It was satisfying to see his eyes seek her when they all returned to the house, triumphantly bearing their catch of several fish.

Phil baked them with gin, Tahiti-style, and they ate them for lunch. Then the yachting party left for Kawau, a pretty island further up the coast where they intended to spend several days exploring before heading for home.

'Come and see us,' Clary said in parting. 'I don't want to lose touch with you.'

'I'd like that.' But she had no intention of following through, because when she left Motuaroha she was going to put the whole visit behind her.

Clary gave her a sharp glance and said, 'Here's our phone number. Do get in touch.'

'Thank you.' She was kind and perceptive, and it was thoughtful of her to let Finley make the first move towards a closer acquaintance.

After they had been waved around the headland Finley heaved a sigh, and said happily and thoughtlessly, 'Oh, lovely peace and quiet!'

Blake chuckled, not at all annoyed by her pleasure at the departure of his friends. 'Pleasant, isn't it? What would you like to do this afternoon?'

Whatever he was doing, but she could hardly tell him that. She shouldn't even admit it to herself. 'Suggest something.'

He grinned. 'Can you ride?'

'Well, I can stay on a horse. I've been informed by those who know that it's not exactly riding.'

'Hmm. In that case we'll take the Land Rover to Shipwreck Bay and I'll teach you to windsurf.'

'I'll have you know I'm an expert at that,' she retorted, nose in the air, 'but I'd love to go.'

Looking back from the wet misery of winter, the days that followed were like memories of another life. When it rained it did so at night, and the days were golden and sweet-smelling, the essence of every connotation that the word 'summer' can inspire. Days when the sky was a deep, burning blue and the clouds like whipped cream, days of heat so tangible that it could almost be touched, days spent carefully sunbathing to toast her slender paleness into gold. She swam in the home bay and windsurfed and walked with the dog along the coast. Other days, she picked pipis with the children and feasted on the small succulent shellfish, learned the names and faces of everyone who lived on the station, and came home tired to spend the evenings talking and reading and listening to music with Blake.

She was completely happy.

As the lassitude left by her illness retreated, she began to realise just how pressurised she had been for years, ever since she had left school. Now, in this time *out* of time, she relaxed and gave herself completely to the lazy enjoyment of each precious moment.

'I'm a total hedonist,' she complained cheerfully from the depths of the hammock.

'Living for pleasure?' Blake looked up from his newspaper. His gaze ran the length of her body, almost insolently appreciative. 'About time. The shadows under your eyes have only just gone and you no longer look as though each step might be your last. However, that dog is getting too fat. You'd better cut down on his intake.'

'Poor Blackie.' She dropped a languid hand over the hammock and was rewarded by a quick swipe from a warm tongue. 'He looks much better, doesn't he?'

'He does. Between you and Phil he's a fair way to being spoiled. Have you decided what to do with him when you get back?'

She frowned, regretting the intrusion of the workaday world in this idyll. 'I'm going to see if he can be happy with me. My neighbour is a dear, she loves animals and she might be prepared to look after him when I'm at work.'

'It sounds worth a try.'

By an unspoken, mutual decision they never discussed her work. Apart from that one forbidden subject they talked voraciously about anything and everything. Their awareness of each other gave an edge to conversation, a sharp thrill to each moment they spent together, yet they never touched. Blake made no attempt to appeal to her through the senses, she did not use the shop-worn tricks of flirtation; they could have been old friends without a sensual moment to remember, except that each time gold eyes met green the memory of those heated minutes smouldered into life.

It was like living on the lip of a volcano. The sensible thing to do would have been to leave, yet the sweet danger of desire held them trapped even as common sense prevented them from surrendering to it.

Finley couldn't go. She learned the rhythms and patterns of farm life, watched as Blake spent some time out on his beloved acres and more shut up in the office coping with the ramifications of an agricultural empire. She could have been lonely, for he was kept busier than most men, but she welcomed the quiet and the peace.

It had been the best two weeks of her life, and the smile she gave him was radiant with gratitude and something else she was unaware of. He smiled back, the angular toughness of his features relaxing into amused affection. At least, that's what she told herself it was. It was safer that way.

'Come for a swim,' he said.

They were by the pool at one side of the house. It had, Blake told her, been designed by his wife. She had done it extremely well but it bore the kind of smooth designer's gloss which tended towards artificiality.

'OK,' Finley said.

Some minutes later they heard the voice of Betty Marchant, the head shepherd's wife. 'Sorry,' she called as she came through the gate, but she did not look in the least sorry, she was bubbling. 'Oh, Blake, I've just had a phone call from Ian and he's got leave for this weekend!'

Blake's powerful back rippled with muscle as he hauled himself over the edge of the pool. Finley's mouth dried; she swam to the steps and slowly, sedately, walked up them. It was swimming which drained the strength from her legs, not the magnificence of Blake's near-nude body as he listened to Betty.

'So we thought a barbecue-cum-birthday party,' Betty

was saying. 'Hello, Finley. My son is coming home on Saturday with about five friends for his twenty-first birthday.'

'That's great.' Finley draped a towel over her shoulders, wishing that Blake would do the same. Like that, as unselfconscious as one of the Greek athletes he resembled, he set every nerve in her body aching with frustration. The water coated him with a shining film which emphasised every muscle, every spare curve and plane, the strength and symmetry of triumphant masculinity.

'Have you spoken to Phil?' he asked now, pushing his darkened hair back from his face.

'I thought I'd better see you first. I don't know whether you have anything planned for this weekend?'

'Only a twenty-first birthday party,' he teased. 'Phil knows she can take as much time as necessary to help you.'

'Thanks, Blake.'

When she had gone he said absently. 'You'd better go and dress, you'll get cold.'

She had shivered, but it was not from cold. 'What does Betty's son do?'

'Young Ian? He's in the army. Betty and Don had reconciled themselves to missing his twenty-first.' He smiled down at her, his lashes spiky with water, his expression mocking. 'You've not been to a party here, have you? Everyone comes and everyone pitches in to help. That's why she's gone to see Phil.'

Betty came back beaming. 'Everything's organised. Oh, this is going to be such fun! Blake, you're a darling. Now, where am I going to get five girls for these friends he's bringing.'

At the peal of laughter from Finley and Blake's grin, she looked bewildered, but a moment's thought had her laughing too. 'Oh dear, it could have been better put, couldn't it? Never mind, you know what I mean.' She beamed again. 'I must go and make a list of things to do and get. Thanks a million, Blake.'

When she left them this time Finley said mischievously, 'I must admit to being a little puzzled as to why you're a darling. Seems to me it's Phil who's going to do the work.'

'Don't you think I'm a darling?'

The lazy note of flirtation in his voice surprised her but she answered in kind, widening her eyes as she gazed soulfully up at him. She even managed to flutter her lashes. 'Of course I do. You know you're irresistible and I'm just a simple maiden—no! Don't you dare! I take it all back. Though I must say I'm rather proud of that simper. It's quite difficult to do.'

Her instant capitulation stopped him from dumping her back in the pool. He didn't even touch her, which was just as well, because for a moment he seemed to be having as much difficulty as she was at making the mental shift back to within the boundaries they had set up together.

'And here was I thinking it came naturally,' he said judicially. 'I'm glad, you look awful when you're doing it. Come on, let's get you dressed.'

As they turned towards the *cabana* he said, 'The reason for the profuse thanks is that Phil will feed us on scraps while she embarks on an orgy of food preparation for this party. She adores giving free rein to her creative impulses. Every refrigerator, as well as the freezer-room, will be jammed with the results of her efforts.'

'I see.' She paced beside him, conscious of the way he always moderated his long stride so that he didn't race away from her. A little raggedly she said, 'She was right. You are a darling.'

He shrugged, saying cynically, 'When you live on an island it pays to be good to the hired help. They can be damned difficult to replace. The men like living here, but most wives prefer lights that are a little brighter. And closer.'

'Well, that's put me in my place. OK, your second name is Gradgrind.'

He picked up the allusion, sending her a little taunting smile. 'Dickens would have found me to be a perfect model of the bloated capitalist,' he said blandly.

She laughed, as he meant her to, and they separated at the doors of the changing-rooms. But, as she showered and dressed, she wondered at the reason for his occasional displays of cynicism. Lisa?

She must still have been frowning when she emerged, because he looked up from his position in the chair and asked immediately, 'What's the matter?'

'Just wondering if Phil knows how you malign her,' she said lightly. 'Scraps, indeed!'

He didn't believe her but he said nothing. They were so very careful not to exceed the limits of their relationship, she thought sadly. They both knew how fragile were the restraints they put on themselves. Sometimes she would look up to catch him watching her, and the brooding emotions she saw in his expression would transform his face into a bronze mask of desire before he had time to control it. And she had only to see him and awareness chased through her body, weakening her with its volatile, consuming fire.

But the last thing she needed was a love affair! Oh, it would be ecstasy while it lasted, rapture and anguish and exquisite, forbidden pleasures of body and mind and soul, but she needed to be totally single-minded. Ahead of her lay two years of extremely hard work, with examinations eighteen months on, and if she was to fulfil her ambitions she had to pass. She knew the pass rate. Forty per cent, which meant that she had to work harder than she had ever done before.

So there could be no time for passion.

And Blake should be looking for a wife, not a mistress. She had spent lonely hours in her bed deciding on the sort of wife he needed. In fact, she was rather proud of her ability to view the matter with such objectivity. He needed a woman brought up in the country, a nice, sensible woman who would find complete fulfilment in her marriage and children and the life on the island. She would need to be good-looking but above all, she should love him with the complete conviction a naturally dominant man like Blake would demand.

It was stupid to wish that she was that sort of woman, that she wasn't lumbered with this inconvenient sense of vocation. It was even more stupid to lie in her bed at night and make up scenarios in her mind which led to aching unfulfilment and profound shame in the morning.

That night, they watched a panel discussion on television between representatives of the varying export industries in the country. When it was over Blake switched the set off, saying, 'That must have been rather dull for you.'

'Not in the least. One thing I regret about medicine is that it's a bit like being in an enclave, we tend to talk only of medical things. What on earth are Nashi pears?'

'A Japanese fruit, shaped like an apple, very crisp and juicy. There is a good market for them but, like all the fruits destined for Japan, they have to be perfect. I've planted some on the Bay of Plenty property to see if we can do it without exorbitant labour costs.'

Finley, who had had no idea that he owned a horticultural property in the Bay of Plenty, said, 'What about goats? And deer? I'm sure the last time I heard anything of either they were noxious pests and government hunters were culling as many as they could from helicopters.'

'Now they catch them from helicopters.' He gave a

wicked, reminiscent grin. 'And very exciting it is, too. I went out after goats a couple of years ago.'

His stories made her hair stand on end, revealing a streak of recklessness which should have appalled her. It did, but she thought she understood it, too. The death of his father had thrust him into power when he was barely twenty, forcing him into a situation where the responsibilities were immense. It was no wonder that occasionally a well-controlled streak of restlessness surfaced, the wild youth of twelve years ago rebelling against the responsibilities he had assumed.

'It's a wonder you didn't kill yourself,' she scolded. 'Jumping from the helicopter like that! I'll bet the attrition rate of goat and deer hunters is pretty high.'

'Oh, they're not fools, and they're a pretty tough breed. It sounds more dangerous than it is. Anyway, didn't I hear one of the boys bragging about how *neat* a diver you are? He told me you jumped from the rocks into Chloe's Pool, and that must be damned near twenty feet.'

She flushed. 'I used to dive at high school, I'm really quite competent. I knew exactly what I was doing. But I didn't know they were watching.'

'They know better than to copy you.' He watched her with hooded eyes. 'You're so small you inhibit my reasoning processes. Sorry.'

'It doesn't matter. I think that must be why I decided to do pediatrics. At least the children don't eye me as if I'm a schoolgirl masquerading as a doctor. If I go into a pub I have to produce a driving licence before they'll serve me! You have no idea how frustrating it can be!'

'Don't I?' He spoke grimly, the framework of his face suddenly prominent. 'Everyone suffers at some time from other's misconceptions.'

'You?'

He directed a flat, cold gaze at her. 'Why should I be exempt? The things money buys are very pleasant, but have you ever considered what it's like to be able to buy anything you want? Friendship—of a sort. Sex. Amusement. A wife.'

Finley's fingers tightened across her suddenly damp palms. She had no idea what to say, but she had to banish that frozen harshness. Her tongue touched her dry lips; she said quietly, 'You're saying that because you're indecently rich, people treat you in a particular way?'

'Recalling your lectures on psychology?' He was far too astute not to recognise what she was doing.

Finley bit her lip, a little angry with him for seeing through her so quickly. 'Well, is that what you mean?'

'I suppose so.' He stretched his long legs out in front of the chair he was lounging in, his big body somehow giving an impression of tension. He was watching her too closely for comfort, as though he sensed her unease and was rather contemptuously amused by it.

'Poor little rich boy!'

That brooding watchfulness vanished. He said appreciatively, 'You're a nasty piece of goods. Tell me that you're not dying to know why I married Lisa and I'll believe you.'

He was altogether too percipient. Finley wrestled with her conscience before accusing. 'You're a demon!'

'I know Marie,' he said calmly. 'She's always been obvious. I married Lisa because she convinced me that she was in love with me and that she'd be happy here. I had already decided that it was time I settled down, and I was prepared to go along with her. God knows, she was beautiful enough to wake any man's libido.'

'Poor Lisa.'

He nodded, watching her from beneath lashes. 'Oh yes, poor Lisa. She found life here unbearably dull, and I discovered that sex with nothing to back it up becomes nauseating. I had no idea how stupid she was! Behind the vivacity and the sparkle there was nothing; she couldn't think, she just reacted. But I didn't wish her dead.'

'I never thought you did.'

He steepled his fingers, surveying her with bright, shrewd eyes. 'No, I know. You're a compassionate soul, Finley. I wish you weren't also a dedicated and ambitious one. When I marry again it will be to a woman who won't kill herself from boredom as Lisa did.'

That hurt, a swift, shattering pang which jagged through her like lightning. That night, instead of indulging her imagination, Finley went over his words, remembering reluctantly the flash of pain in his eyes when he spoke of his wife, his cynical comprehension of his motives, his refusal to pretty up his actions.

He was a complex man, subtle and difficult beneath the surface charm, and he had warned her off with an honesty which was almost brutal.

Finley wept, because it was such a waste to feel this singing in the blood and know that it was for a man who could never be hers.

'Lust,' she taunted herself, but her heart whispered another word beginning with the same letter.

CHAPTER SEVEN

'No,' said Phil, very firmly.

'Look, I know I'm not the world's best cook, but I can follow instructions!'

Unmoved, Phil set her hands on her hips and looked Finley over. 'You are also several pounds too light and you still tire too easily. You're not going to spend all day on your feet in this kitchen and still end up with the energy to party half the night.'

'But——'

'No. Blake said that you are to rest.'

'God has spoken!' Belligerently, Finley thrust her chin forward.

'He has indeed. He's also quite capable of making sure that you do as you're told.'

'By tying me to a bed, I suppose,' Finley said mutinously.

Phil gave a sudden knowing grin. 'I doubt if *rest* would be what he had in mind in that case,' she said, and laughed as colour flamed across Finley's cheeks.

'You,' she retorted loftily, 'have a dirty mind.'

'Realistic. Practical. Now, why don't you go and have a swim and a shower, wash that pretty hair and have a rest? Then it will almost be time to start getting ready.'

'I feel useless. And I am twenty-six, not ten years old.'

'Start acting like it and I might treat you that way,' Phil returned smartly. 'It's better to feel useless than exhausted. You don't have to prove anything to me. You'll spoil things for the others if you have to go home early tonight, or if you go wan and limp like you do when you've done too much.'

Finley regarded her steadily. 'That was a low blow. Devious, even.'

'As well as being realistic and practical, I have a son. Being devious comes naturally, believe me.'

Smiling, Finley gave up and retreated to the pool, languidly swimming lengths until the heaviness in her limbs encouraged her out. For a short while she lay beside the pool, listening with drowsy pleasure to the sounds of the island, the harsh cry of a gull breaking into the high sweet clarity of a skylark's song, an impatient whicker from one of the horses, and the unrestrained bellow of a beast further up the valley. And over all, the soporific zither of the cicadas' chorus, plaintive and soothing, which blended so well with the anticipation humming in the air.

When the skin on her arms and back began to tingle she trailed up to her room and followed the plan Phil had outlined, managing to dry her hair before succumbing to lethargy on the bed.

It was almost dusk when she awoke and the pleasant hedonism of the day was replaced by an excitement which turned her eyes into green jewels set in a glowing face. As she brushed the smooth mass of hair and applied make-up, Finley told herself that there was no need for such anticipation. It was, after all, only a party. Normally she didn't like them much!

But her body and her heart knew what her mind refused to recognise and, beneath the fever-bright glints in her eyes, there was a slumbrous, patient confidence which would have terrified her had she understood it.

Instead she allowed her gaze to drift almost casually over her reflection, until, with a strange little shrug, she turned away from the slender figure in the mirror. The dress suited her, a plain thing relying on its cut and the slither of silk to make its point.

'Now, no howling or carrying on,' she said to Blackie, scratching his poll. His tail wagged but there was a wistful quality in his gaze as it followed her out of the room.

Blake was waiting at the bottom of the stairs, lounging against a door with the indolent grace which seemed so paradoxical in a man of his size. In the shadowed hall, his hair gleamed molten gold and she could feel the blaze in his eyes as he watched her come down the stairs.

Excitement took wings within her, beating like a bird in her breast. Solemnly, slowly, she came down towards him, her eyes imprisoned by his. The beautiful line of his mouth tensed; his lashes drooped and through them she saw the authentic look of desire.

As he held out his hand he said under his breath, 'You burn in my heart, Finley . . .'

The words were gutteral, involuntary.

'Oh, don't,' she whispered, fighting the sensations which licked across her nerves.

He held her hand to his mouth, kissing first the thin fingers and then the soft palm. She stared at the dark line of his lashes, the strongly etched lineaments of forehead and cheek and jaw, the arrogant, acquiline symmetry of bone and flesh which gave him an intense, masculine beauty.

Her hand trembled. He straightened and said huskily, 'You're an enticement I cannot resist. If I were a poet I could tell you what it does to me when you look at me like that and I see all the promises of the sirens in your eyes. Forbidden—and impossible—and so potent that every night I dream the dreams of the damned.'

The stark sincerity in his deep voice stripped the words of everything but a fierce, elemental hunger.

Finley's fingers curved along the hard jut of his jaw. 'Yes,' she said with sombre intensity, and pulled his hand to her mouth.

He jerked it free as if her lips were poisoned. For long seconds the air between them vibrated with tension. Then, as if a shutter had come down he retreated into himself and without the need for any more words they walked out of the house.

Half-way down the drive he pointed out the flat bar of cloud along the horizon which indicated a change in the weather. Finley asked questions and was treated to an interesting, amusing little dissertation on weather signs. Agreeably she quoted a few old clichés garnered from her subconscious, and then they were at the house.

Betty and Don Marchant greeted them enthusiastically. With them was a tall young man who was the guest of honour; he gave Finley a dazzled, respectful glance before shaking Blake's hand with even more respect and a very obvious liking.

It was an extremely enjoyable party. The Marchants had a lovely garden and a wide terrace, and a keen instinct of hospitality; everyone had come to determined to enjoy themselves, and they did. As the sky flowered into scarlet and gold before dimming to green and the immense, deep blue of night, there was enough talk and immoderate laughter to satisfy even the most apprehensive of hosts. There was flirtation and teasing and dancing, and then dinner was set out. Over the superb spread there were toasts and the ceremonious cutting of a cake by Ian, who grinned and blushed and made a witty reply to Blake's speech.

After that, the children were tucked off to sleep in various rooms and the music became softer and more romantic. Blake put down his glass, took Finley's from her and set it beside his, then with a smile which did not reach his eyes, took her into his arms.

It was like going home. Sighing, she rested her forehead against his shoulder. The tension in him was duplicated in her, but she forced herself to relax. This was what she had been waiting for. He was so big, the heat from his body enfolded her; he held her as if she was the most precious object he had ever touched. She found his eyes and they were blank, as expressionless as his face, but beneath the cheek she turned in a cat-like gesture along his chest his heart beat frantically, in time with hers.

When the tape ended he released her without looking at her, and for the rest of the night seemed content to let her be whirled off her feet by the five friends of the guest of honour. She had a duty dance with each of the married men as well, and danced with the two unmarried hands on the station; she talked, she laughed, she even flirted a little. She must have behaved quite normally. Nobody stared at her as if she was mad, yet, as each sentence left her mouth, she had no idea of its meaning and her smiles were as empty as her words.

She did not look at Blake, she knew that he did not look at her. But she felt his attention, knew that his whole concentration was as focused on her as hers was on him.

At last the party began to break up. Children were picked up, farewells said. Blake carried a soundly sleeping Mark a hundred yards or so, and Finley felt as though her heart was clamped in a vice. He should have children of his own; he would be a good father, tough but fair, with the gentleness of the truly strong.

Then there were just the two of them walking back to the homestead, close but not touching. The cicada chorus had died with the sunset, but crickets were singing and, high above the trees behind the house, a little breeze crooned and played beneath the trembling stars.

Finley yawned and stumbled, throwing out a hand. It was caught and she was swung up into his arms.

'Hush,' he said, and her protest died instantly.

'I can feel your heart beating.' Now, why had she said that, and in such a smoky, provocative little voice?

'It's a wonder you're not deafened by it!'

'I'm going home tomorrow.'

His hands tightened on her yielding body. 'It's too late. If you had really wanted to escape you should have gone that first day.' There was a moment of taut, strained silence before he added grimly. 'Except that I think I would have followed you. It happened in the first five minutes, my heart.'

'I know.'

His arms lifted his burden higher. Finley closed her eyes and listened to the thunder of his heart against his cheek. She knew what was going to happen. She had known since she walked down the stairs. Dreamily, she thought that her life had been a preparation for this, and the blood sang exultantly through her veins heating her skin and glowing in her lips.

She kept her eyes closed, even when she was placed on a bed. It had been pulled back and the sheets were crisp and fresh, smelling of sunlight.

'Are you asleep?' he asked softly as he slipped her frivolous little shoes from her feet.

'No. I'm shy.'

She felt his fingers touch the button at her breast. Laughter and desire melded in his voice like two sorts of gold. 'Shall I take you to your own chaste little bed?'

'No,' she whispered, peeping beneath her lashes.

One lamp glowed behind him so that he was silhouetted, the harsh, proud lines of his face implacable against the golden glow. In spite of the laughter in his voice he was not smiling. He was looking down at the hand which rested with casual possession on her breast. He looked chillingly remote.

Finley covered his hand with hers. Her heart leapt like a wild thing. She said nothing but in her grave eyes there was the permission he seemed to need.

'I always knew it could be like this,' he whispered, as his mouth came down to hers.

She expected a fierce and hungry loving, braced herself for it, but his mouth was warm and gentle, waiting until she could stand it no longer and her lips parted in invitation. Only then did his arms slide about her to pull her off the bed, as the force of his kiss bent her head back, and he explored her mouth deeply and with passionate intensity.

For a moment she was passive, until an answering desire exploded through her, and she responded with a wild passion which was a challenge and a temptation. A deep little sound died in her throat and she gave herself up to the sensual pleasure of tasting him, of making her own discoveries.

She was shaking when at last he lifted his head, but she turned her head into his tanned throat and kissed the pulse there, taking an innocent, sensuous enjoyment in the taste of salt and his own particular scent. With hands which shook, she freed the buttons on his shirt and pushed it back over the breadth of his shoulders, her wide eyes filled with the smooth expanse of him.

'You are—magnificent,' she said, putting a finger on one of the taut muscles.

He laughed beneath his breath and watched with narrowed eyes as she turned her head and touched her tongue to his shoulder; she lifted an incredulous face as he shuddered.

'Take your dress off.'

She bit a tender lip.

'Humour me,' he muttered. 'If I touch you I'd probably rip the thing to shreds.

She almost believed him. He looked dangerous, his drawn face fierce and deliberate, merciless in the dim warmth of the light.

Carefully, deftly, she stepped free of the narrow gold silk, rejoicing at his sudden harsh breath. Unbidden, under that hungry gaze her nipples peaked in the small curves of her breasts. The whisper of silk was loud in her ears as she tossed her dress on to a chair; she undid her bra and dropped it. Then, impelled by a wanton impulse she had never before experienced she ran her hands from the waistband of her french pants to her breasts.

He said something, a statement of need so blatant that

she blushed from her hands to her forehead, and he smiled, and said, 'Come here.'

Hawk's face, wolf's smile. What am I getting into? she thought in sudden, useless panic, her hands falling to her side in tense little fists.

He caught her and pulled her between his legs, holding her with ruthless hands. 'It's too late,' he said.

She began to struggle, gazing into his merciless face with dilating eyes. He held her hands behind her, forcing her shoulders back and down, arching her back. He lowered his head and his mouth closed over the tip of her breast as his free hand pushed her pelvis forward, thrusting her against him.

Finley gasped, pierced by desire. Immediately he released her, and she staggered, head falling forward. He caught her and, a moment later, she was in bed between those crisp sheets and he was undressing. She watched avidly, apprehensive yet entranced, her eyes roaming the intimidating muscled power of his body. Her responses were running wild, throbbing through every cell in her body like liquid fire.

When he came into the bed beside her she whispered his name in a high, distant voice, as her eyes glazed into wildness.

A long time later, when he had reduced her to mindless surrender so that all her fears were dispersed, he moved over her. She moaned softly and opened for him, accepting that first tentative probe with tense anticipation. He was so big—and then he took her, made himself the possessor of the sweet fire within, and she wondered why she had ever feared this.

'Finley,' he said thickly, restraint etched deep in his countenance. Her eyes flew open. She locked her arms across his back, glorying in the weight of him on her, the scent of their arousal in her nostrils, his taste on her tongue as her teeth closed on to his shoulder.

'Oh, God, don't,' he groaned. 'You make it impossible for me—to control——'

Her tongue lingered on the place she had bitten. 'I don't want you to be in control,' she whispered, mimicking that slow gentle thrust of possession with her hips.

The gold in his eyes flamed into a conflagration. His lips drew back from his teeth in a primal snarl. 'Siren,' he gasped, and that iron restraint shattered into desperation.

His arms were like steel beneath her back, his body an instrument of pleasure so acute it was pain, demanding a response as unguarded and explosive as his. Finley's hands clenched on to muscle hard as rock; her nails scored his skin as she cried out, and then her body tightened and she was racked with sensation, waves of ecstasy which set off a shuddering release in him.

Then there was a period of golden satiety, of the slow spiral back to reality, and some time during it Finley discovered that tears were sliding down her face in silent streams. Blake had her cradled to his shoulder and was stroking the tousled strands of her hair back from her face, making an occasional soothing noise as she gulped and choked the tears into cessation.

'Here,' he said, proffering a handkerchief.

She blew her nose, wiped her eyes and stuffed the handkerchief under the pillow, saying weakly, 'How do people manage to survive that? I'm sorry, you must think I'm crazy.'

'Not at all,' he told her politely. 'Sensory overload, that's what you're suffering from.'

She gave a watery chuckle. 'Does anything ever throw you?'

'That did,' he said bluntly. 'Now go to sleep.'

She did, sliding immediately into an unconsciousness which was too profound to last. When she awoke it was in the false light before dawn. She had expected to wake in Blake's arms but, during the night, she had wriggled back on to her side of the vast bed and was in her usual position, flat on her back. She turned her head, seeking reassurance, but he was not there. A sudden fear had her swivel her head, and she saw him. He stood in the window, one arm holding the curtain back, a big dark silhouette against the fainter darkness outside.

Finley said, 'Blake?'

He turned his head. He wore trousers and nothing else, and he looked impossibly withdrawn, as though he had found some remote place where she was not welcome. He said, 'Good morning.'

She lifted herself on one elbow, trying to pierce the darkness so that she could get some clue as to his mood from his face. 'Is it?' she asked drily.

He let the curtain fall and came silently back to the bed. 'Suffering the usual post-coitus doubts and insecurities?' he asked cynically.

'No doubts. No regrets, either.'

He lay down beside her on top of the blankets, linking his hands behind his head to stare up at the ceiling. Outside, a rooster gave a signal for dawn. It sounded sad and lonely. Finley lay very still, wondering what thoughts were forming in that clever mind. I love him, she thought wearily. How stupid.

'Finley, will you marry me?'

She knew what she had heard, but she said, 'What!' just the same.

'I want you to marry me.'

He spoke coolly, without expression or emphasis. No hint of emotion showed in the striking profile. Finley didn't even have to consider her answer.

'No,' she said quietly. 'It wouldn't work, Blake, you know it.' When he made no reply she continued quickly, 'I know virgins are pretty rare nowadays, but the price doesn't come that high.'

It was a misguided attempt to keep things light and

sophisticated, and she wasn't surprised when he replied angrily, 'Give me some credit for finesse, my dear. I'm not trying to buy your virginity with a wedding ring.'

Finley rather thought her heart was breaking. Pain was a stone in her chest, but she managed to say, 'I'm flattered, of course, but——'

'*Flattered?*' In one deadly movement he turned and imprisoned her with the weight of his body, a forearm on each side of her shoulders. He smiled, and real fear kicked in her stomach. 'Flattered,' he repeated thoughtfully.

His weight and the pressure of his arms tightened the blanket so that Finley could not get her hands up from beneath it. The slight mounds of her breast were flattened and tender. She lay quiescent, her eyes enormous in her small face as they searched his. Her innocent comment had unleashed the devil in him. She could see it in the quirk of his lips, the narrowed, fierce slivers of gold beneath his eyelids.

'Now why should an honest proposal of marriage flatter you?' he said silkily, and lifted himself slightly so that he could ease his knee between her legs. He looked disinterested, as though he were conducting an experiment with no emotional capital invested in the result.

Finley stiffened. 'You don't have to force me,' she said bleakly. 'But if it turns you on ...'

He closed his eyes, but not before she had seen the flash of pain in them. 'The perfect mistress,' he said harshly, before his face came down to the vulnerable hollow of her throat.

They lay like that a long time, Finley stroking the bright hair with a loving hand.

At last he said, 'I'm too heavy,' and moved so that she was free.

'Are you going?'

'No,' he said, smiling, and slid his trousers off and came beneath the sheet and took her sweetly and sensuously in his arms.

She kissed his chin and his ears, followed the reckless line of his jaw with her kisses, explored the virile splendour of his body with an open fascination which brought the breath hard and fast through his lips. Outside, the dawn warmed the smiling island and the crickets handed over their shift to the cicadas, but inside, behind the curtains, they inhabited their own night world. She whispered of love and desire, her slurred, husky words erotic messengers.

He knew what she was doing. Although he lay still he was not passive. His body reacted with subtle and wonderful signs to her tender ministrations until at last he groaned, 'My God, you have the finest natural talent for this. How do you know I like that? . . . oh yes . . . yes, my heart . . .'

It was an admission and she smiled a secret woman's smile. I love you, her heart sang but she said nothing, flowing over him as he lay open to her in his enormous bed.

'Nobody else,' he muttered, sweeping a hand up to cup her breast. 'It has never been like this before, never.

"From tawny body and sweet small mouth
    Feed the heart of the night with fire." '

Finley trembled and whispered, 'Oh, my love, my dearest love. . .' turning her face into the warmth and security of him, surrendering in a heady welcome which was its own reward.

He said her name, twice, and then neither spoke again. When at last they lay twined together in exhaustion she slept, to wake in the same position, locked against him, her small slenderness lost in his arms.

'Swinburne,' she murmured, loathe to let the night go. 'Do you like his poetry?'

'Not particularly, but I must admit some of it sticks in

the mind.' His mouth moved against the skin of her shoulder.

> ' "For a day and a night Love sang to us, played with us,
>
> Folded us round from the dark and the light . . ."

I have to get up, my heart.'

'And I.' She buried her face in his neck, folding her shaking lips. 'I didn't know that it would be like this.'

The cynicism she so disliked hardened his voice. 'I'm sure there's a quotation to cover that, too, something on the lines that everything has to be paid for one way or another. I suspect that for us the payment has only begun.'

The cloud which had been in the sky the night before had crept past them during the night but, as he had predicted, behind it the weather had changed. The dreamy, sensuous ambience of summer was gone. The sky was as clear, but it had a polished look; the sun shone as brightly but the air was brisk rather than drowsy.

After breakfast, Blake left to draft a mob of cattle from the other side of the island. She did not ask him to stay. He was just as bound by discipline as she. He worked harder and longer hours than any of his employees.

So Finley packed and went around to say her goodbyes, startled by the open regret with which her decision was greeted.

'But of course, we'll be seeing more of you,' Betty Marchant said cheerfully, her mild eyes curious.

Smiling with painful determination, Finley returned a non-committal answer but, as she walked back to the homestead, she was hurt by the knowledge that she was not likely to see anyone from Motuaroha again.

Nor the house, serene in its golden stone, unless she saw it from the sea. Perhaps she might see the outline of the island if she travelled north from Auckland but she doubted that she would be able to pick it out from the other islands in the gulf. And she would never come back. Motuaroha and all who lived on it belonged to the past.

Why couldn't you have been a different person? she demanded bleakly of the absent owner.

But the notion was ludicrous. Blake loved his land, drew sustenance from his acres and his work. Just as she did. He was a farmer, he could not live in Auckland, and she could live nowhere else but in a city.

Hot tears scalded her eyes. Under Blackie's worried gaze she collapsed on to a chair on the terrace and wept silently.

'Nothing good comes of meddling with Blake's affairs, but the last time I walked past a weeping woman in this house she died a few hours later.' Phil's cool tones were completely at variance with the concern she couldn't hide.

Finley sniffed inelegantly and wiped her eyes. Her voice, though ragged, was staunch. 'You needn't worry, I'm not given to grand gestures or suicidal impulses.'

'Suicidal impulses weren't Lisa's style, she was too greedy, but she was certainly a great one for grand gestures. That's how she died. Stupidly.' Phil sat down, watching Finley warily. 'She was such a stupid woman, you have no idea. She used to complain because he wouldn't spend half his life escorting her round the social life she thought she deserved, she nagged and whined and cried, and she thought she could get away with it because she was stunning to look at. Why did you decide to go home? I thought you were going to spend another week here.'

Finley said nothing. After a moment Phil said exasperatedly. 'It doesn't seem fair!'

'Life is frequently unfair,' Finley returned. 'I can't stay, my work means too much. I'd end up like—well, like Blake if he'd gone to live in Auckland.'

Into her mind there came an image of him as he had been the day after they met, half-naked as he rammed earth in around the post. He could have sent someone else to do it, it probably hadn't been necessary to work like that. Yet he had done it with a fierce, elemental enjoyment in his skill and his strength, and afterwards he had sat beneath the tree and looked out over his kingdom and his love for it had been so plain that she should have left the island that day. Instead, lured by a hunger she had barely understood, she had stepped into the forbidden country of his heart, and like many trespassers, she was not the only one to pay the price.

'No great damage done,' she said in a metallic voice. 'I've had a marvellous holiday and I'll have a week to get over it! It will give me time to organise some sort of baby-sitter for our canine friend here.'

Blackie wagged his tail and jumped up to lick her chin.

'You've decided to keep him?'

'Yes.' Finley took his paws and guided him back to the ground. 'I didn't realise how much I needed a dog until he chose me.'

'I wish things had worked out,' Phil said. 'I've known Blake all my life and believe me, a better man it would be hard to find. He deserves—oh, forget it!'

The ferry left the hotel at three in the afternoon. At a quarter past two Phil's husband presented himself.

'Doesn't look as though Blake's going to be able to make it in time,' he said awkwardly. 'Something must have come up. I'll take you over if you're ready.'

'Packed and ready to go.'

In accordance with immutable law, the trip back seemed much shorter than the drive out. Finley responded to the cheerful conversation directed her way and watched the smiling acres go by, grass and fences and plantations, prosperous, beautiful—the true love that held Blake's heart.

Once within the hotel boundaries she relaxed. He was not going to come. It was cruel, yet by far the kindest way.

'Here we are,' Phil's husband announced unnecessarily, drawing up in the paved courtyard with a flourish. 'I'll just get your bags out—what the hell's going on in there?'

From behind the doors a small commotion resolved itself into a prostrate man and a group of people. Finley jumped from the vehicle and raced in, realising immediately that the man who knelt by the recumbent form was just as alarmed as the rest of the onlookers.

'Oh, thank God!' That was the manager, fervent and worried. 'I think it must be his heart. He just collapsed.'

Finley lifted an eyelid and checked the ominously quiescent artery in the neck before beginning external heart compression.

'Have you rung the police?' she demanded.

The manager nodded vigorously. 'The helicopter's on its way.'

'Good. There must be someone here who can do mouth-to-mouth?'

One of the waitresses knelt, nodding as Finley said, 'One breath to every five pressures, OK?' She turned her head to the manager. 'How long will the helicopter be?'

'About twenty minutes.'

'See if there's anyone else who can do mouth-to-mouth, will you? Cardiac massage, too.'

'Sure, fine.'

'And get rid of these people.'

Half an hour later, as she walked off the lawn which served as a helicopter landing pad, she pushed hair which was damp with sweat back from her face with a hand which shook slightly. It had been a relief to turn the patient over to the duty doctor in the chopper and to know that she had given the patient a better chance of survival than he would otherwise have had.

From behind her the manager said, 'Thank God you arrived. He just dropped like a stone. I didn't know what to do.'

'Perhaps you should take first aid lessons? Don't you have a nurse in evidence?'

'Yes, but would you believe it?—it's her day off. She went to town this morning.' He nodded at the ferry which was turning into the bay. 'She'll be on that.'

'I think I'd organise a replacement on her days off,' Finley suggested drily.

He nodded, frowning, then said with something like relief, 'Oh, there's Blake. I saw him come a while ago but he seemed to disappear when the chopper came down.'

And there he was, so alien to the luxurious atmosphere that he should have looked completely out of place. Instead, clad though he was in dusty working clothes, he dominated, drawing admiring, speculative eyes.

Finley's love broke into life inside her, expanded, filled her with a fierce possessive pride.

'Hi,' she said, unable to hold back the smile that radiated her face.

He smiled back but his golden eyes were watchful. 'You look very competent when you're being a doctor.'

'Thank you.'

He touched her cheek then turned to the manager. 'Organise a bathroom for Miss MacMillan,' he commanded. 'You can tell me what happened and how you plan to avoid a repetition while she's showering.'

'But the ferry,' Finley protested.

He looked at her. 'It will wait.'

It did, too. Perhaps he owned it as well as the hotel!

Twenty minutes later he walked beside her down the jetty. No one seemed annoyed at the unexpected delay, but Finley was too troubled to have noticed.

'If I ring you, will you go out with me?' he asked.

'I think it's better not to, don't you?'

The bright head moved in a decisive nod. 'Oh yes, I'm

sure it's far more sensible. But if I ring . . .?'

'No,' she said, harshly, quickly. If she allowed this to drag on it could only end in desolation and despair. She had made the right decision, she simply had to stick to it.

He was quite impassive, the strong features rugged in the bright sunlight, but something leapt into life beneath his lashes and she could feel his rejection of her stand as clearly as if he shouted it.

He said nothing, however, and they came, unspeaking, to the ferry. A man stuck his head out of the cramped wheel-house and called a cheerful greeting to Blake, his interested gaze travelling from Finley's shuttered expression to Blake's, and back again.

'How's Rosa?' Blake asked after replying.

'Fit as a buck rat. Yourself?'

'Could be worse.' Suitcase in hand, he swung on to the boat, tossed a comment to a deckhand which made him grin broadly, and held out a hand to Finley.

'I can manage,' she said resolutely, but she obeyed the silent summons and let him help her on to the ferry. Blackie jumped across and sat down with his head alertly poised on one side. Her suitcase was passed over to the deckhand.

'Take care,' Blake said quietly, and stepped back on to the wharf, striding along it without a backward glance. Finley made an odd little grimace, then went through the door into the main cabin. She sat down, keeping her gaze towards the gulf. Blackie lay on her feet and went to sleep.

CHAPTER EIGHT

IT WAS warm in the cabin, and cheerful. The gulf was a little more choppy than it had been on the way across, but the brisk breeze drove the yachts with speed and gallantry, so that the waters seemed filled with their sails, glowing in all shapes and colours and sizes, swaying and straining towards home.

Islands slid by, beautiful, beach-bordered, and then there was the olive-green bulk of Rangitoto the interloper, hurled from the fiery depths of the earth a few hundred years ago. Excursion boats threaded their way between yachts, a massive container ship dwarfed all about it, making its passage along the empty corridor towards the docks, and launches and runabouts left creamy wakes behind their noisy engines.

At the wharf the ferry pilot said, 'If you wait a minute, I'll help you up with that suitcase. The stairs are pretty steep.'

Nice of him, Finley thought, and waited patiently while the other passengers got themselves and their luggage off. He grinned at her, swung on to the steps and shifted the suitcase into his other hand.

'Been staying with Blake, have you?'

'Yes.'

'Nice place he's got. Wouldn't be the same harbour without the Cairds at Motuaroha. His grandfather was an old tartar, could eat nails for breakfast—no trouble. Blake's just as tough but he doesn't show it as much.'

'I had a marvellous holiday.'

He grinned again and guided her through the building to the pavement. 'Ah, here we are,' he said, indicating a waiting taxi. 'Blake thought you might have a bit of

136

trouble getting one so I organised it over the radio.'

He cut short Finley's thanks by speaking to the driver, who handed him a sheet of paper to sign. 'There you go,' he said. 'All signed for. See you.'

'Goodbye. Thank you.'

Finley gave the driver her address and climbed into the taxi. Blackie scrambled in and sat pressed against her legs, his muzzle on her knees as he stared apprehensively up at her. After the tranquillity of the island Auckland, even in its Sunday afternoon guise, was too big and too busy. No matter that eveyone was dressed in casual clothes, that the people heading for the buses were laughing and sunburned and weary, they seemed alien, almost threatening. Finley wanted nothing more than to be back with Blake.

When the taxi drew up in a leafy street not far from the hospital she felt a tired relief mingled with depression. Her half of the house seemed minuscule after the homestead's spacious rooms. Small and very ordinary. Without much enthusiasm she pushed windows open to dispel the stale air. The lawn needed mowing but the garden was gay with hibiscus and dahlias.

A knock on the door heralded Sue Browning from the flat next door. 'What happened?' she demanded, warm brown eyes alarmed as they scanned Finley. 'You're supposed to have another week. Remember what happened last time you went back too early! Are you all right?'

Finley smiled. 'I fell in love,' she said simply, 'and I ran.'

Sue's mouth dropped open. Blackie stopped bristling to advance. Still staring, Sue extended her hand for him to sample. He sniffed politely then sat back on his haunches.

'Come and have a cup of peppermint tea,' Sue urged. 'You look whacked. Bring Old Faithful with you.'

Sue and her husband Brett were both teachers, she at

the local primary school, he at one of the city's high schools. They were saving frantically to buy a house, putting off their plans for a family until they were financially secure. Sue had decided that caffeine was poison, so she served her long-suffering husband and friends a variety of herb teas. Some were pleasant, others strictly for the dedicated.

'Brett's out sailing,' Sue said as she led the way next door. 'You might have seen him on the way in.'

'Him and ten thousand others.'

'Meet Pippa, the latest member of the Browning family!'

A sinuous cream and brown kitten was draped along the back of an armchair, gazing at them with mad, slightly crossed eyes.

'Blackie—no!' But, although both women watched with trepidation, Blackie advanced soberly towards the chair. When only a short distance away, he sat down and regarded the Siamese kitten with his head on one side.

'I thought dogs chased cats,' Finley muttered.

'I thought cats ran away from dogs. Hey, look at that! I don't believe it!'

For the kitten leapt down from the chair, picked herself up from a rather undignified landing and advanced enthusiastically towards Blackie. The entranced dog lowered himself to kitten level, his tail wagging furiously. The Siamese began what could only be construed as flirtation.

'Talk about shameless!' Sue began to laugh. 'It looks as though we have a pair of soul mates here.'

It did indeed. Sipping peppermint tea both women watched as cat and dog went, side by side, to sleep. Sue described how she had bought the kitten, and then Finley told how Blackie had acquired her, and gave a brief account of the past two weeks. An account which Sue interpreted with devastating accuracy.

'Boy, you certainly chose a big one, didn't you?

Everyone knows about the Cairds, of course. I remember the publicity when the hotel was opened. Great fanfares. Not much about your man, he's apparently a man who values his privacy, but quite a lot about his wife. I remember the fuss when she died, too. Lots of juicy speculation.'

'He's not my man.'

'No?'

'No!'

'Suit yourself, but if that's the impression you want to give, don't say his name too often. Your voice takes on a distinctly tender intonation. What went wrong, love?'

'Oh Sue, there's no future. He won't live anywhere else, and I've got my life planned!'

Sue's brows lifted. 'Got as far as futures together, did it? Quick workers, both of you. Two weeks, Finley! You can't learn to love anyone in two short weeks.'

'I know.' Finley drained her cup and set the saucer defiantly back on the table. 'I've told myself that, said all the sensible things. But—oh, Sue, it was incredible. We looked at each other, just like in the films, and that was it.'

'That was attraction.'

'It was a recognition.' A bitter little smile made her older. 'Whatever it was, it's impossible. If I gave up my career I'd go crazy.'

'Oh, no, you couldn't do that. Not after all your hard work. What about him? Couldn't he sell—well, no, I suppose not. But he doesn't have to live on the island, surely? He's some sort of tycoon, he's got interests all over the place. Couldn't he buy ten acres on the outskirts of Auckland and look after his empire from there?'

Finley shook her head. 'He needs space,' she said simply. 'It would be like blindfolding an eagle. I couldn't ask him to make such a sacrifice, not when I'm not prepared to make a similar one.'

'I see.' Plainly Sue didn't, but she realised that Finley

was very close to exhaustion. 'In that case, you're just going to have to forget him. Or get him out of your system, whichever is the easiest.'

'Once I get back to work it'll be easy.'

'Of course it will.' Sue was good at pretending, too. 'Now, have another cup of tea, and I'll make you glad you stuck to an easy option like medicine instead of taking your life in your hands by teaching.'

Finley listened to tales about Sue's eight-year-olds, and laughed, and then Brett came home and they decided to go out and eat pizza for dinner, and with their help and some red wine Finley was able to push her despair to the furthest limits of her consciousness.

Somehow she managed to get through the next week. She wrote polite little bread-and-butter letters and posted them with relief, then threw herself into redecorating her bedroom, stripping old wallpaper and hanging new, repainting, even buying a new spread and curtains.

'I like it,' Sue enthused, covertly surveying not the room but its owner. 'Sophisticated. That spread picks up the colour of your hair. And the green is exactly the right contrast to those lovely tawny shades. You look like a wood nymph.'

'A nymph? She's tried to camouflage herself out of existence.' Brett was not romantic. 'I can only see you when you move. Still, it's very fetching. The only thing wrong is the dog. Accents of black are not suitable. Why not trade him in for a corgi?'

Both women regarded him with horror while Blackie grinned and scratched at an itchy spot on his ribs.

'Blackie,' Finley said brightly, 'is the small brother I never had.'

'And Pippa is the little sister Blackie never knew.' Sue looked at both animals affectionately. 'What are you having for dinner, Finley?'

'Dinner?'

'Dinner. You know, food, stuff you eat. It keeps you

alive. You don't look as though you're having more than a nodding acquaintance with it at the moment. Let's go and get Chinese.'

Finley capitulated. She knew that starving herself was no sensible way to behave. Some women emptied the refrigerator when they were unhappy; misery made her feel a faint but unmistakable nausea which put her completely off food.

It had to be better when she went back to work.

It should have been. As usual, she was stretched to the limit on duty and the paperwork hadn't diminished. Nor had the cruel number of hours, or the stress of knowing that lives and welfare depended on the decisions she made. Everything was as it used to be. Everything but Finley, and she was withering away with a broken heart.

At first she thought that will-power could overcome it, and indeed, she was able to prevent the shaming bouts of self-pity by force of will. But the empty, weary despair which shadowed her days and made intolerable the restless nights could not be banished. Sometimes she thought she could taste it, heavy and acrid on her tongue, and whenever her eyes fell on a tall blond man her heart leapt in sickening, jarring supplication. She felt raw, as though some necessary part of her had been torn away and the wound left exposed and bleeding.

She was suffering all the agonies of love unfulfilled. What made it worse was her realisation that Blake was probably suffering too; it did not help to discover that the career for which she had given him up failed completely to take his place.

There must be an ending, she told herself, as summer slid into autumn and the memories of those weeks on the island began to recede behind the realities of everyday existence. This pain must go, it could not continue to eat like an acid into the fabric of her life.

'Come and sample some grapes with me,' she invited Sue one hot afternoon.

'Oh, don't they look delicious! Where did you get them?'

'The parents of one of the children who was discharged today own a vineyard. They brought in a huge box and these are my share.'

'Mmm. Beats an apple for the teacher any day. I heard your phone ringing for ages this morning after you left.'

'They'll ring again.'

But that night she found herself staring at the telephone, willing it to ring. When it remained obstinately silent she was irrationally convinced that it had been Blake trying to contact her. She found herself looking him up in the directory; there were not many Cairds in it, but his name was there.

It would be crazily stupid to ring Blake, but she had Clary Caird's number . . .

'No,' she said angrily, startling Blackie. With a shaking hand she replaced the directory. If she contacted Clary she would hear news of Blake, and that would destroy all her efforts so far. She had gone this far, she had to continue.

'You don't look as though you've got over your pneumonia fully,' one of the house surgeons observed the next day.

Finley was used to parrying observations like this. 'Perhaps I should prescibe myself a tonic.'

He grinned. 'Better yet, why not come to a party we're giving tomorrow night?'

'Oh, Tim, I——'

'You need something to take you mind off whatever it is that's giving you those dark circles under your eyes. I've seen our beloved registrar looking at you askance.'

The registrar was a pleasant, rather austere woman whose pragmatism was underlined by a warm compassion which could never have been mistaken for sentimentality. Finley admired her and was a little afraid of her.

'Then I'd better start wearing cover-stick,' she said gloomily.

'To hide the circles? You could try it, I suppose, although nothing will convince me that she doesn't see right through to the marrow in your bones.'

'You're probably right.'

'About this party . . .'

Finley made a sudden decision. 'I'd like to come, thank you.'

Normally she would have enjoyed herself very much. Tim's parties were always fairly low-key affairs with superb food and music, and a lot of cheerful conversation. His wife saw to the music, Tim the food.

This one was well up to standard. Finley drank a glass of white wine then switched to soda water, flirted companionably with a couple of unattached males, one an old friend from medical school, the other a friend of a friend who stood out in the mainly medical gathering by being a horticulturalist from the Bay of Plenty. By asking him questions about his work she felt ridiculously as though he was a link with Blake. He was a kiwi-fruit grower and he would have liked to monopolise her all evening, but, ignoring his patent interest, she introduced him after a while to another woman and drifted on.

A pleasant evening, she decided as she drove home. One she would repeat. Too much solitude, however much she craved it, was unhealthy.

That night, for the first time since she had come home, she slept soundly. When she woke she told herself that she had been right, it was only a matter of time, the process of healing had begun.

It was, therefore, disheartening that the pain remained just as intense. Although she now functioned more like her usual self the sensation of despair, of aloneness, was always there. Slowly, with a kind of appalled reluctance,

she was forced to admit that Blake had become necessary
to her. She longed for the physical magic of their
lovemaking but as much, she yearned for his companionship, the strange completeness it gave her to be with him.
There was the mental exhilaration of their conversation,
the warm laughter, the rightness of it all.

She thought of him incessantly, yet when one evening
she picked up the telephone receiver she did not at first
recognise his voice.

'Finley?'

'Yes. Who—*oh*!'

'Would you like to have dinner with me some time next
week?' he asked bluntly.

Her fingers clenched white on the receiver. She should
refuse—she had to refuse. But there were limits to will-
power. 'Yes,' she whispered.

There was no change of intonation in his voice, no
relief or pleasure. 'Are you free Friday night?'

'Yes.'

'Good. Any preferences? Ethnic, French——?'

'No. No, I don't mind.' Provided I'm with you.

'I'll see you around seven. Goodbye.'

She had plenty of time to castigate herself for her
weakness but, although she tried, her heart was not in it.
For days, she moved in a dazed, incandescent glow of
happiness which lit her small face to radiance.

On Friday her eyes were glittering and she had to use
foundation to tone down the flush of excitement across
her cheekbones. Since coming back she had not bothered
to have her hair cut in its usual smooth page-boy, and it
was now far too long for sophistication, so she swept it
into a tidier knot than her working style, holding it in
place with silver combs she had inherited from her
mother.

Because the evenings were cooler than they had been
on the island, she wore a light velvet blazer over a
matching dress of rose pink silk. As extremely high heels

made her look ridiculous her shoes were medium-heeled but they were slender courts, a far cry from the strappy little sandals she had worn on Motuaroha.

When the doorbell rang she checked her desire to rush to open it. Just as well, because it was Sue who stood there.

'You do look lovely,' she said, beaming. 'I came to see if you'd like us to baby-sit Blackie.'

Blackie had settled very well to life with Finley, probably because he spent a lot of time with Sue and Pippa.

'He doesn't howl any more.' Finley wavered.

'He might start again,' Sue said cunningly. 'Anyway, Pippa adores it when he comes over. I'll get his sheepskin, shall I?'

'I can——'

'Don't you dare. Black dogs hairs will not add anything to *madam's ensemble*.' She slid past Finley and emerged a few seconds later with dog and sheepskin. 'There, all is under control.'

Her glance moved past Finley, settled with eager interest on a point beyond. 'Oh, boy,' she breathed inelegantly.

Anticipation leapt to a sickening crescendo in Finley's heart. She turned, smiling to cover her confusion, and there he was, bigger than she remembered, infinitely more attractive, in clothes which managed to be both elegant and casual while they outlined his flagrant masculine appeal.

If either of the other two noticed that Finley's voice wobbled as she made the introductions neither indicated it. Blake used that relentless unconscious charm and Sue went under like a drowning woman.

'Nice neighbour,' Blake commented, as he slid Finley into the front seat of a superb Jaguar.

'She's a darling.' When he got in she feasted her eyes on him, throwing caution over her shoulder like a good luck charm. Her hungry heart fed on his presence with delicate greed; she could never have enough of him. She could worry about tomorrow's painful approach when it came.

Her recklessness lasted through drinks at a small luxurious restaurant in Parnell, where the waiters wore red cummerbunds with their dinner jackets and the tables were adorned with roses which effused the perfumes of old Persia. Something in the décor reminded Finley of Granada and Moorish Spain, of the hidden passions of Araby. She felt Victorian and romantic and reckless.

They talked softly but intensely, conveying much more than the words, so lost in each other that the arrival of the food came as an interruption and a shock.

Normally Finley would have relished the superb meal but it could have been hamburger for all she noticed, the wine a sharp red instead of being a French name. In fact, she probably wouldn't have noticed if it had been water.

'You're thinner,' he said, the hard-bitten features revealing nothing.

Her shoulders lifted. 'I'm back at work.' It was no answer and they both knew it. 'Anyway, you look as though life has been hectic for you, too.'

He gave her an ironic smile, his eyes lingering on her mouth. 'I've been missing you.'

'Good,' she said, giddiness making her incautious. 'I'm glad I'm not the only one to have suffered.'

'But you knew that we would before you left me, didn't you?'

She nodded, her lips twisting. 'We should never have been so foolhardy.'

'Coward,' he taunted softly.

'Well, what if I am? I didn't want to fall in love with you.'

The wine glowed scarlet in the thin crystal goblets. It captured the light and transformed it into a trembling pool of fire on the table which bathed Finley's fingers as she drank recklessly. The room was cleverly lit to enhance the romantic, sensuous environment; lamps warmed Finley's hair into brilliance and emphasised the harsh masculine character engraved in Blake's face. He looked at her and she knew how a specimen must feel, pinned out and exposed.

Very quietly he said, 'Is there any possibility that you might be pregnant? I took no precautions that night. I couldn't think past the fact that I had to have you or go mad.'

Was that the reason for this unexpected invitation? Chagrin almost made her snap an answer but she saw the hunger and need he was trying to hide, and she said slowly, 'No, I'm on the Pill. There are other reasons than contraception for using it.'

He made no reply but she saw something, quickly hidden, in his expression which made her ask incredulously, 'Did you hope that I might be?'

'It could have made a decision easier,' he said, as though the words were sour in his mouth.

She shook her head. 'Blake, that's no basis for marriage. Besides, I can't—I *won't* give up my work.'

He must have recognised her determination because he said nothing more on that subject. Tentatively, she broke the tense silence by relating an incident which had occurred at the hospital a few days before.

He listened, even smiled at its hilarious conclusion but, when she had finished, he said wryly, 'I find that I'm jealous of the fact that your life has no place for me, my heart,' and steered the conversation into other channels.

The rebuff was pointed and hurtful. Finley would not forget it but she forced herself to overlook it. She had tried so very hard to forget how superb a companion he was, well-read, with an incisive, sceptical way of exploring issues which contrasted with her more emotional attitudes, and now every sentence he spoke reinforced his effect on her. They struck sparks off each other; he made her think, probing for the reasons to her statements so that she found herself defending her views with more depth than she had ever used before. He was, however, no bigot. Although he had strong views on most subjects he was prepared to listen and evaluate a contrary argument. He was fascinating. He was brilliant. He was her lover, and she grew drunk on his presence.

Over coffee she looked up and the awareness streaked like sheet lightning between them, all-consuming, fiercely elemental.

'Let's go,' he said on an odd, thick note.

Out in the car he asked curtly, 'Do you want to go on? To a night-club?'

'No.' Her answer came swiftly, without time for thought.

Against the light from the street lamps his profile was hewn granite but, as he set the car in motion, she knew that she had pleased him. Neither spoke all the way back but as he switched off the engine she asked, 'Coffee?'

Again he smiled. 'Why not?' he said.

She made the coffee and they drank it, talking quietly while the undercurrents ran deep and strong between them. Then Blake took her empty cup and set it beside his, turning to slide his arm about her shoulders and pull her across his lap. He did not kiss her immediately, although he must have been conscious of her need for his caresses. For long moments he surveyed her, his forefinger tracing the soft line of her lips, while the passion he had kept subdued all evening took mastery of his features.

At last, when her nerves were screaming with frustration, he said with an odd little sigh, 'That smile has haunted me since you left, your smile and your green eyes, and your quick brain and your generous heart. You left loneliness behind you.'

'I brought it with me,' she whispered, capturing his

hand so that she could kiss the inside of his wrist. It was warm and sinewy, and she thrilled to the feel of his life-force pumping through the blue veins.

'Did you? Doesn't your precious vocation fill your life as completely as you thought?' As if to purge himself of anger he lifted her so that he could reach her mouth with his own, and forced it open with casual mastery to search out the deep, warm places within.

'I love you,' she whispered when he lifted his head, the blatant savagery of the kiss exciting her into recklessness.

He smiled a little disbelievingly and kissed the words away. Behind her closed eyelids her pupils dilated, almost banishing the green fire. Suddenly, fiercely, her body arched in supplication.

'In time, in time.' The words were slurred and slow but, beneath them, she heard an elemental satisfaction. 'We have all night, my heart, my lovely one. All night, to do whatever we like.'

Her lashes flew up. A strange, feral little sound escaped her throat and she insinuated her hand through the front of his shirt. At that moment she hated him because he was still completely in control. It became imperative for her to reduce him to the same abject need which swamped her. So she called on primitive, long-hidden instincts, her mouth curving into a blind, siren's smile, and across the heated width of his chest her fingers were light and tantalising as they stroked through the light dusting of hair to the taut skin below.

He watched her with narrowed, intent eyes, his mouth an inflexible line above the strong chin. But she felt his heart miss a beat and then begin to pick up speed, and that feline smile deepened and she nuzzled her face into his chest, finding a flat male nipple with her teeth through the fine material of his shirt, and moistening it with her tongue.

He muttered something, it could almost have been a

curse and, ruthlessly denying her the choice, pushed her dress to her waist with shaking, impatient hands. She wore only a half-slip beneath it, so that she was exposed to his heated gaze. Trembling, she watched as his hand stroked towards the small pink tip of her breast. Passion, fierce and primitive and mindless, surged through her and she twisted, pulling ineffectually at his shirt.

He laughed beneath his breath and stood as effortlessly as if she were weightless, his mouth over hers silencing any protests. Her mouth flowered under his, her small hands gripping tightly in case he set her down to soon.

'I like carrying you,' he said, as he shouldered his way into her bedroom.

She drew a long, shuddering breath. 'Because it makes you feel big and strong?'

He reacted to the taunt in her words with a mirthless smile. 'I *am* big and strong,' he said and slid her slowly, deliberately, the length of his body so that his arousal was patently obvious to her. 'I don't have to prove it. You feel good in my arms, sleek and small and graceful, as if you had been made to fit me.'

Slowly he knelt, kissing her throat, the tight hollow of her navel as if it were her mouth, pushing her dress and the skimpy little slip to her ankles. 'You fit me perfectly,' he said deep in his throat.

Finley gasped and threaded her fingers through the pale glimmer of his hair to hold that tormenting mouth against her breast. She wanted him so much that her body was aching with hunger, yet a strange tenderness held her still.

'I love you.' The words were wrung from her and she tried to silence them in his hair, but his lashes lifted against her sensitive skin.

'And I you,' he said as though each syllable hurt. 'So much. So much, my heart . . .'

He welcomed her fumbling attempt to undress him, the gold of desire blazing in his heavy-lidded eyes.

Passion darkened his skin, pulling it tight over the magnificent arrogant framework of his face so that all emotion was stripped from his expression. Only the sensual line of his bottom lip exposed the warmth she knew existed behind the stark mask of desire.

When at last he stood with her, all powerful grace and muscled strength, she said very simply, 'You are beautiful.'

'And you are the woman ...'

His voice trailed away. The muscles moved in his throat as he swallowed, and he said harshly, 'Get into bed,' and when she did he came down beside her and with hands that shook began to re-learn the slender contours of her body.

He was experienced and clever, he knew what to do to make a woman receptive. Yet Finley realised that for him this was a new and uncharted territory of the heart. When his mouth touched her breast it was like the first time for him, every sensation washed new and untarnished like fresh-minted gold, transformed by the strange alchemy of love.

And for her the raw sexuality of this mating, wild, fiery, exhausting, was as fulfilling as that tender, careful initiation in his bed on the island. Led by sensations and emotions which absence had intensified she incited him, she gasped and moaned and gave herself to him with such primal urgency that his control snapped, and he took her with a passion akin to ferocity, the desperation she needed from him.

Yet, she thought dreamily as she lay against him in the aftermath, listening to their hearts slow down, there had been no cruelty in their loving. Even at the height of the sensory storm which had enveloped them he had been considerate with his great strength, desiring to give as much pleasure as he received.

He had succeeded, oh, so well. Pleasure, she thought drowsily, her mouth moving softly over his warm damp skin. She had drowned in it, sobbed with a surfeit of it, moaned her pleasure to the moon and shuddered at his deep, gasping cry as their combined pleasure soared into ecstasy.

'How the hell did you manage to stay a virgin so long?' he asked on a yawn, running a completely possessive hand down her body.

She laughed and kissed his chest. 'I didn't know it was like that. If I had I might have succumbed years ago.'

'Really?' Where he summoned the energy from she didn't know, but he flipped her on top of him, his hands cupping her face so that he could scan her face. 'I rather got the idea that you had made a moral choice.'

'Well, I thought it was too, but I think it might have been straight self-protection. After my mother left my father she embarked on a series of affairs. I think she hoped to find her one true love but as I saw her grow more and more disillusioned I decided, that's not for me.'

'Love affairs, with or without sex, shouldn't end in disillusion.'

'You're the expert on those,' she said cheerfully. 'Apparently my mother didn't know the rules. Or she expected too much. Whatever, I never wanted anyone enough to break my own rules.'

'Not even the man you were engaged to?'

She smiled sleepily. 'No, not even him. Looking back, I think that's probably why he wanted to marry me. He was used to quick conquests and I suppose it was a blow to his ego when I refused to go to bed with him. So he wooed me and we got engaged.'

'Thereby satisfying that ego. He sounds like a conceited fool.'

Finley gave a choked laugh and dropped her head on to his chest. 'I think he must have been. I started to regret it straight away. He wanted a big wedding, all the trimmings, and he started hinting that I give up medicine. I found the parties he went to incredibly dreary, all business-orientated and false, and it wasn't long before I realised that he was selfish and totally single-minded when it came to getting ahead.' She yawned. 'I'm sure he'll turn up one day as the ruthless head of his firm.'

'Unlikely,' Blake said. 'Self-servers rarely get to the top echelons. They don't see clearly enough beyond their own selfish interests. I feel sorry for the man.'

'Why?'

'Because he was the first to run against that dedication of yours. I think the reason you won't marry is the same as the reason you wouldn't go to bed with anyone; you use your work as an excuse to avoid intimacy.'

The idea was laughable, but she was too tired to refute it. Sleepily, she murmured, 'Then what am I doing here?'

'You met someone who was safe.' He tucked her beside him, pulling the sheets and blankets up. Through waves of exhaustion she heard him finish grimly, 'Because there is no way we can marry, you and I. So you can enjoy an affair with me, safe in the knowledge that I won't expect you to give yourself entirely to me. After all, mistresses aren't expected to surrender everything. That's strictly for wives.'

She should have told him that he was wrong but, even as she began to compose an answer, she was asleep.

CHAPTER NINE

SHE woke to sunshine across the room, the smell of coffee and no memory of those last words. Smiling, stretching, she discovered quite a few well-used muscles as she hauled herself up in bed preparatory to getting out of it. Through the half-open door she heard the scritch-scritch of Blackie's nails as he came towards it. She didn't hear Blake but he was in front of the dog, carrying a tray.

Suddenly shy, she pulled the sheet up to cover herself and smiled rather mistily at him. He wore his trousers and nothing else. He looked gorgeous.

He set the tray down and bent to drop a kiss on her nose. 'Why is there no food in your kitchen?'

'Oh, I don't eat much,' she said vaguely.

'So I notice. I've made some toast, after cutting off a rather impressive culture of penicillin from the side of the loaf. There's honey in the pot.'

He had set the tray with her pretty china and added a spray of summer jasmine in an egg-cup. The sweet, cloying perfume of the flowers blended with the aroma of the coffee. Finley was suffused with a sensation of well-being so perfect that it was hard to contain.

'How did Blackie get in?' she asked, smiling radiantly at the dog as she buttered toast.

'I heard your neighbours stirring half an hour or so ago, so I went out and renewed our acquaintance. Blackie seemed eager to make sure that you were still intact.'

'Oh, lord,' she said, amusement and chagrin blending in some disharmony in her countenance. 'Bang goes my reputation!'

'Does it matter?'

Something in his intonation stilled her knife. An upward glance revealed that he was watching her far too intently. 'No,' she said lovingly. 'Of course it doesn't. Have you had anything to eat?'

It was the right answer. He relaxed and came to sit on the side of the bed and, while Blackie watched wistfully, she fed him toast with brown manuka honey, then they drank the coffee. After that she showered, choosing a narrow dress cut like an over-length shirt to wear, and found that he had done the dishes. So, while he used her tiny shower and changed into clothes he had in a case in the back of his car, she made another cup of coffee and they drank that on her minuscule terrace at the back. The sun beat down with autumnal fervour and bees hummed busily amongst the dahlias.

'I'm free until about two-thirty this afternoon,' he said after he had helped her wash those few dishes. 'How about you?'

'Yes.'

'What would you like to do?'

She linked her arms around his back to rest her cheek against him. He felt large and warm and very solid.

'I don't care,' she said dreamily. 'Just as long as we're together.'

'I'd taken that for granted.' His voice reverberated in his chest. 'Would you like to visit Morgan and Clary? They're not far from town.'

Disappointed, she managed to nod, but a long finger tilted her chin and he laughed softly, his eyes gleaming with satisfaction. 'No?'

'I like them immensely but——'

'But you'd rather be alone with me.' The satisfaction softened his expression as he kissed her, taking his time. 'Mmm, you taste like honey and roses and love. Come on, I'll take you to the Waitakeres.'

What she wanted to do was stay here with him, but she sensed an inner restlessness in him which kept her tongue still. He was too vital to be at peace in the confines of her small flat.

So they drove up the Waitakere Hills, the range which is a rampart on the western horizon of Auckland. There they walked for some miles down one of the excellent forest trails, admiring the big *kauri* trees and trying to imagine the grandeur which must have existed before the bush had been cut over.

Every moment with him was sweet, yet Finley was on edge, wondering what exactly it was that he wanted from her. Was it an affair, with exclusive rights to her bed each time he came to Auckland? Last night he had said that he loved her, but he had not repeated it.

And what had he meant by those last cryptic remarks made as she was falling asleep? They had come back to her now and she wanted to tell him that he was wrong, that she did not use her work as an excuse to prevent the surrender that marriage entailed, but one glance at his shuttered face forbade any discussion of it.

She tried very hard to enjoy their walk, laughing at Blackie's determination to tow them down every side-path in pursuit of exotic and exciting scents, but her smile became strained and it was almost a relief when at last he said, 'Time to go back.'

That he was aware of her feelings had been almost certain; not much escaped those keen eyes. It was with a small shock, however, that Finley heard him say, 'What's the matter, my heart?'

She stared out of the window at the heavily bushclad sides of the road with their discreet gateways indicating houses tucked into the folds of the hills, and blurted, 'I don't know what you intend to do!'

He made no pretence at not understanding her. 'When you left Motuaroha I was determined not to see you again,' he said evenly. 'Common sense convinced me that that was the safest way to go. Unfortunately, it was easier to decide than to do. What do you want to do?'

She had not bitten her nails for years but she found now that she was chewing on her little fingernail. Horrified, she dragged it away and hid the maltreated hand in her lap.

'I don't know,' she said, wishing that he would make the decision, wishing that she didn't have to accept any responsibility. 'Do you want an affair?'

He smiled with sardonic appreciation. 'We're already in the throes of one. Do you want to be my mistress, Finley, welcome me to your body and bed whenever I come to Auckland—always providing that my trips across don't clash with your duty hours?'

She bit her lip but, after a moment, said carefully, 'It seems the only possible way of handling things, doesn't it?' Before she had time to consider the wisdom of it she continued, 'You were wrong last night when you said that I was afraid of marriage.'

'So you were awake. I didn't say exactly that. I said you were afraid of intimacy.' His voice was hard; he was apparently unmoved by the distress she wasn't able to hide. A muscle tightened in his jaw. Derisively he finished, 'I don't *blame* you. The idea scares the hell out of any sensible person. At the risk of sounding like an amateur psychologist I'd say you decided at the time of your parents' divorce that you weren't ever going to lay yourself open to that kind of pain. Your mother's subsequent actions reinforced that conviction. So you became absorbed in your vocation. It will always be there, it won't let you down.'

'If that were right, I wouldn't have let you get to me,' she said defensively, because it made a kind of truth.

'You thought you'd be safe, you'd always been safe before. Just as I thought I was safe. By the time we discovered that fate had played a gigantic joke on us, it was too late. Neither of us were thinking clearly enough to do the sensible thing. Then we made love, and suddenly we realised how great the danger was. You fled back to Auckland and I couldn't get you off the island fast enough.'

'But it didn't work,' said Finley sadly.

'No. And we're stuck with it. Why should we expect to have it all? I already have more than my fair share of the world's gifts, so do you. Beauty and brains and character rarely go together. Why should we expect to have the whole fairy story, marriage and children and happiness? Nowadays those whom the gods love don't die young, you doctors see to that, they merely discover that the more you have the more you are denied. The law of averages defeats us all, one way or another.'

It was a bitter little speech, yet there was no note of anger in his voice, merely a vast and cynical tolerance which hurt more than any anger could have.

He stretched out a hand and gripped the two in her lap for a second before asking, 'Shall we try it then, and see how things go?'

Afterwards, she never understood why she asked him. Perhaps the words came bursting up from her subconscious, impelled by a need to know, all the stronger for being unwelcome and unacknowledged.

'Have you done this before?' When he slid her a stabbing, sideways glance as though he could not believe that she had asked him, she finished doggedly, 'Conducted a long-term, long-distance affair?'

His cynicism was mocking, wounding. 'Oh yes, I've done it before. Do you want to feel that this time it's different, my heart? Sorry, I can't give you guarantees like that.'

It hurt, as he had intended it to. Tears glinted in her hot eyes as she stared down into her lap.

'I'm sorry I can't be the woman you want me to be,' she said almost inaudibly.

Beneath his breath he said something succinct and savage, then his hand covered her knee in a caress as fierce as it was short. 'My patient little love, I shouldn't bore you with my complaints. I accepted some years ago that the world is not run for my exclusive benefit. I should have the grace not to rail at fate.'

He pulled into the car-park of a shopping centre. 'Let's get something for lunch.'

They bought pâté and French bread, an assortment of cheeses including a wedge of imported Stilton, some olives and a superb fruit tart.

'Have you any wine?'

She nodded, smiling. 'What's left in the cask I bought for my last party about four months ago.'

'My God!' His horror was not faked, but amusement lurked in the mock-severity of his expression.

He bought French champagne, dry and palest gold, and two bottles of an Australian red which he said were to start her cellar. 'I can't drink stale cask wine. I have a palate!'

'Most people have.' She said it pertly, glad because he had banished the dark mood of a few minutes ago.

'Not my sort. Mine is a cultivated, sophisticated palate, trained to detect the faintest nuances in wine and food.'

She had to laugh at the smug, almost sanctimonious note he managed to infuse into his nonsense. She loved it when he was like this, teasing, making no attempt to hide his pleasure at being with her.

'What conceit! How did you acquire this superb palate?'

'Great natural talent, of course, and some time spent drinking rough red in France. It either refines or atrophies the taste-buds very rapidly. Come on, let's go back and eat. Toast is not enough to keep a man my size going for more than an hour.'

They ate lunch picnic-style on the tiny terrace, the time passing too fast, too easily, minutes slipping into limbo like pearls off a string.

'Come here,' Blake said softly, when she finished her glass of champagne.

She went to him, insulated against the world in a haze of golden pleasure.

'I think I'm drunk,' she said cheerfully, slipping into his lap.

'How does it feel?'

'Funny. I like it, but not as a regular thing.' She snuggled into his shoulder. 'You don't have to ply me with alcohol, you know. I'm quite amenable to any advances you care to make.'

His chest lifted with his soft laughter. 'You're a shameless hussy. I see what you mean about not being responsible after several drinks. I'd like to take you into a bedroom and keep you there for days—weeks! Probably months.'

'Until you'd slaked your lust,' she said knowledgeably.

'It seems an unlikely possibility.' He spoke with sombre emphasis, tipping her face so that he could see her expression. 'I've never felt like this before.'

She nodded, gazing up at him with such open adoration that he closed his eyes against the radiance. 'I love you,' she whispered, kissing the warm strength of his throat.

They sat in the sunlight, the sexuality which crackled between them disciplined into a joyous, wordless communication. He smelled faintly musky; no after-shave, just his own distinct and individual scent. Perhaps that was the odour which scientists said reacted on the unconscious to produce lust.

Perhaps that was what love was, a gigantic cosmic joke

perpetrated by that part of the brain which functions outside the bounds of logic and common sense.

No, love was a kind of rapture, a deep upwelling of joy because he was alive and she had found him. If I never see him again, she thought drowsily, it will have been worth it, because I have learned what love is. What she felt for him transcended the shop-worn terms used to describe love and desire; she needed new words, expressions as new and fresh and unalloyed as her love.

With a shock of recognition, she realised that even in this moment of supreme joy she was using her old trick of distancing herself from emotion by building a barricade of words between it and herself. She knew why, too. It was because she was afraid that by accepting her emotions she was opening herself to pain. Her defence mechanism lay in the adjectives she searched for; she was not going to hide behind them any longer.

'I love you,' she whispered, pulling up his hand to hold it to her cheek.

His fingers curved, then relaxed. He traced the delicate dark arches of her brows, the soft fringe of lash, the vulnerable temples. Slowly, imprinting the form and tactile qualities of her face on his brain, his fingers moved across the curve and hollow of cheek, down the straight slim nose, lovingly across the soft sensitive lips. His thumb slid between them and ran along the slightly crooked line of her top teeth.

Finley caught his wrist and held it still, pressed small, open-mouthed kisses down the lean hand to the mound at the base of his thumb. There she hesitated, then bit delicately yet with unmistakable erotic purpose.

She felt the sudden clenching of his body with languorous pleasure, opening her eyes to the narrowest of slits so that she saw the transfixed hunger in his face.

'Finley,' he whispered. 'You know, don't you, what you can do to me? You like it. Little cat, warm and sensuous and daintily, explicitly greedy. I feel the electricity run through you whenever I touch you and I catch fire. I want to take you and keep you . . .'

He rested his forehead against hers, holding her hands still. Finley sighed voluptuously, listening to the thick, impassioned words as her hands registered the racing beat of his heart.

'I didn't know I could be so belligerently, jealously possessive,' he confessed. 'I long for you all through the days, and at night I lie in bed and I imagine you there with me as you were that night, small and sleek and golden, with your sweet moaning voice, giving me everything I asked for with such whole-hearted generosity, and I can't sleep, I can't rest . . .'

His hands hurt her. He pushed her head back across his arm and kissed her with a fierce stirring need which answered the hectic desire his words had roused.

He stood up and she whispered, 'It must be almost time for you to go,' and he laughed mirthlessly and replied, 'Oh, to hell with it! I decided to go back on the afternoon's ferry because I wanted to prove that I could leave you, I didn't need you. It's not important any more. You can have this victory along with all the others.'

Later, when he had left, and she was letting in an indignant, reproachful dog, she remembered the bitterness in that final remark. Like her, he had been content with his life before she had exploded into it. They had been secure, armoured against emotion and pain. Now they were unprotected. Along with the singing joy and the golden web of sensuality there walked fear and regret, and that bitterness which she had deflected on to fate, and he had fixed on her.

'Those old Victorian poets knew something,' she told the interested Blackie. 'Him and his Swinburne. What about Fitzgerald?'

Blackie sat down and grinned at her. She gave him a

rueful smile, touching a finger to her tender lip, declaiming:

> ' "Ah Love! could thou and I with Fate conspire
> To grasp this sorry Scheme of Things entire,
> Would not we shatter it to bits—and then
> Re-mould it nearer to the Heart's Desire!"

There, how's that for a good self-pitying rail at fate?' Blackie walked past her and made for the sheepskin rug which was his power base and refuge. Once there he turned around twice and lay down, peering in a commiserating way through his shaggy fringe.

'You don't like the Victorians? Don't tell me I've a Philistine for a dog? Or perhaps you are a thoroughly modern dog and it's me who is the Philistine.'

The nonsense helped a little to ease the pain. ' "I'm a love lorn woman," ' she said, quoting another Victorian, Dickens, but her voice broke on the last word and she had to go and wash her face.

After that, she went into the bedroom and stripped the tumbled bed, throwing the sheets into the washing-machine and remaking it so that no subtle scent of their lovemaking clung to it to torment her with memories.

The next day Tim, the house surgeon, said, 'You look a lot better. Boyfriend show up?'

'Chauvinist! Does it have to be a man?'

'It usually is,' he said somewhat gloomily. 'Or a woman.'

He said no more, and although she watched him on and off for some days, it was without result. He looked tired, but then so did they all. As far as she knew his marriage was as happy as most. His wife was a few years older than he, a very elegant, sophisticated woman with no pretensions to domesticity. Not that it mattered. She had an excellent job as a lawyer, and she and Tim had always appeared very happy.

You're imagining things, Finley told herself scornfully as she settled down to the vast pile of paperwork which was a fixture on her desk. It was later than usual when she arrived home and the day had clouded over but it was still warm for the time of year. The dankness of winter couldn't be too far away, unless they were going to have one of the rare golden autumns which lasted well into winter.

Sue met her at the back door, holding out a basket of folded clothes.

'Oh, you darling, you brought them in!'

Sue grinned. 'It looked as though it was going to rain. Oh, look, aren't they sweet!'

Blackie and Pippa the kitten embarked on a wild game of chase around the kitchen. Stepping carefully, Finley invited, 'Come and have some orange juice while I indulge in some sinful coffee.'

'Have a good weekend?'

Not taken in by her elaborately casual air, Finley smiled. 'Very good, thank you.'

'Is that all you can say? What an absolutely gorgeous creature! When he smiled at me my toes went all funny.'

Finley laughed but something was lacking, and it showed. Sue asked gently, 'Have I put my foot in it?'

'No, of course not, but oh, Sue, it's such a mess!' Finley lifted miserable eyes. 'I miss him so much, it's hell, and I wonder why I've been so stupid! Blake says it's greedy to want everything, and I suppose it is, but it seems so unfair that my work, which means so much to me, should stop me from having the man I want.'

'It's not your work that stops you,' Sue said, 'The decision to stay working was yours. Your work hasn't forced you to make it. You don't want to give it up.'

'Well, that's unfair too.'

'That you should have to be the one to do the

sacrificing? I agree. It's all very well to say that he couldn't live in Auckland, but that sort of mystical attachment to the land sounds pretty pretentious. Almost as though it's a ploy to use when the little lady wants marriage.'

Finley gave her a startled look. From Sue, that was more than a little fierce. 'With anybody else it might be, but not Blake. I saw him there.'

'Tell me about it.'

As she squeezed oranges Finley said thoughtfully, 'It's like life must have been in a country district fifty years ago. They make their own fun, it's a real little community, close-knit and—and——'

'Claustrophobic?'

'Oh no! Well, perhaps, a little. Although they have the hotel, and the ferry calls once a day. And they have the phone, and television ...' She fiddled with the juicer, suddenly aware of thoughts she had been repressing so firmly that she hadn't realised their existence. 'I suppose it is isolated, but that's part of its charm,' she said slowly. 'And it is Blake's home.'

'And Blake, though gorgeous, is the dominant male epitomised, the sort of man who expects his wife to give up everything and follow him.'

Finley sighed. 'He is the kingpin, the one they all look to. And he loves it. He needs a wife who is prepared to love it too.'

'Has he asked you to marry him?'

'Yes, but it's impossible.'

'Well,' Sue returned deliberately, 'I won't say you've made the right decision because I rather think that you already know it. You have worked too hard, you're too dedicated to give it up for any man, however sexy and fascinating and exciting he is.'

Finley nodded, allowing a glossy sweep of hair to hide her expression. Carefully, she poured the orange juice over ice, added a sprig of lemon balm and handed it to Sue.

'If suffering is inevitable,' she said lightly, 'I suppose I should learn to enjoy it. Perhaps it will make me a stronger character.'

Sue eyed her with a worried frown. 'I doubt it, you're well-enough equipped in that department already, but I do most earnestly believe all this chatter about soul mates, one perfect man for each woman, to be so much romantic fluff. I love Brett very much, but I know that there are any number of men out there I could be just as happy with. In a different way, but happy. Attraction is not exclusive—lord, I meet men I fancy like mad! Respect and liking and affection are just as vital, if not more so, and there are plenty of excellent marriages based originally on one or more of those qualities, rather than on sex.'

'I know.' Finley poured the coffee and led the way into the small sitting-room. They sat down and watched the two animals dotingly as they frolicked for a few minutes.

Then Sue said, 'Yes, you're sensible enough to understand that. I know common sense doesn't help much when you're suffering from a violent attack of passion, but it's a great help when it comes to not ruining your life! Enjoy him while you've got him, and remember him with affection, but don't tear yourself into shreds for something as lovely and evanescent as a rainbow.'

The coffee tasted bitter in Finley's mouth. 'You're no romantic, are you?'

'I'm a practical romantic. I believe in passion and desire and love at first sight, I just don't believe that they are good bases for marriage. To me, marriage is a commitment, two people agreeing that from now on they are going to work towards a common goal. It means children, and I suppose it's because I'm a teacher that I believe that when children come on the scene they deserve the best you can give them, and that does *not* mean a father who has pressganged their mother into leaving a job she loves and is good at and needs. And don't ask me how you can combine a job and a family because I don't know!'

She laughed and gestured derisively at herself. 'Note the soap-box. It's always there, ready to be activated at an instant's notice. Sorry.'

'I like to hear you. Such blazing sincerity!' Finley mocked gently. 'You are being a bit unfair to Blake. He hasn't tried to pressgang me into anything.'

'If he wants you enough he'll try,' Sue said with great conviction. 'It's in the nature of the beast. Those big, gorgeous, macho men can do their utmost to be unbiased and modern and liberated, but deep in their innermost hearts they're throwbacks to cave days. They see women as creatures who, while bright enough, are too slow and too weak to hunt mammoths safely, and who have to be protected from bears and sabre-tooth tigers and things that go bump in the night.'

Finley grinned. 'How did you deduce all this from such a short acquaintance? You're a mind-reader, perhaps?'

'Oh, I'm incredibly clever. Actually, I think it's rather sweet. Secretly, they worship women as the carrier of the next generation.'

The thought of Blake worshipping anything made Finley open wide her eyes. 'You think so? Blake is not sweet. If anything, he's dangerous.'

'I believe you,' Sue said emphatically. 'However, I'll bet you he's got that dynastic streak a mile wide. Anyway, I must pick up my cat and walk or my lord and master could well beat me for being late for dinner.'

'Oh, more than likely,' Finley retorted drily. 'What are you having?'

Sue smirked. 'How should I know? He's cooking it.'

She left an empty space behind her, one which Finley

tried to fill with the preparations for her own dinner. She ate it slowly, reading the newspaper, then settled down to catch up on some reading, sighing as her hand hovered over a travel book from the library. Very firmly, she picked up a heavy medical tome and immersed herself in it.

Five hours later she fell into bed, her brain numbed and exhausted. Sleep claimed her at once but when she woke in the half-light of dawn she lay thinking over what Sue had said.

Had she been correct? Was this just the age-old chemistry between a man and a woman based on nothing more lasting then sexual attraction?

Every instinct in her heart cried out in protest, but she overrode the urging of the sentimental side of her nature and forced herself to examine the situation with a brain clear of emotion. Oh, the chemistry was there all right; a small reminiscent smile pulled at her mouth and she stretched indolently as a cat. But there was more than that, fiercely persuasive though it was. They liked each other, they possessed the same sense of humour, they could talk to each other. She respected him for his intelligence and his freedom from bigotry, and he enjoyed her swift brain as much as her mother had deprecated it.

Lying there listening to Blackie's dreams as the sun struggled through clouds, she made a decision. She would not look to the future at all. She would live from day to day, not worrying about the inevitable end to their love affair. And she would put the thought of marriage firmly away from her.

Her parents had divorced because her mother could not adjust to the narrower horizons of a small country town; Finley knew only too well what results mismatching could have on the protagonists, and innocent bystanders. She was strong enough to survive the pain that would come when Blake tired of her. And eventually the pain would go, leaving her free.

It was late that afternoon that she noticed Tim. He was sitting at his desk, staring down at the papers there but not working; he had, she realised, been still for the last ten minutes. His expression was stark and frightened.

Without thinking she got up and went over to him, touching his shoulder, saying his name.

He lifted his head, looking at her with blank eyes.

'Tim, what is it?'

He gave his head a peculiar little shake as though her voice had recalled him from unknown place, then said, 'Nothing,' in a dead voice. After a moment his eyes focused on her worried face. He stretched his lips in a parody of a smile and said 'I just don't feel too well.'

'You'd better go home,' she suggested very gently.

'There's nothing to go home to,' he sad. 'Therese has left me.'

'I see ... I'm sorry.'

'So am I.' He frowned, pulling himself up from the pit he had been lost in, and said wearily. 'Why don't we have a drink together tonight?'

She didn't want to, but the bleak misery still lurking in his eyes implored her to consent. 'Yes, I'd like that.'

They had the drink, carefully avoiding the subject of his wife, and then Tim suggested a film which the club at the university were running. It was one Finley had always wanted to see, but she would have gone with him if it had been on her least-wanted list. Tim was clinging to her company as an antidote to the empty house, which was all that he had to go home to, and she was worried about him.

'I'll have to change,' she said. 'I'm grubby.'

'I'll come and get you. No sense in the two of us taking our cars. I'll see you at your place in ten minutes, OK?'

'Ten minutes? Well, it will take me a little longer than

that to change, but you can have something to drink while you wait.'

He arrived almost immediately after her, so she sat him down with a cup of coffee while she effected a rapid change of clothes in her room. He appeared somewhat cheered by her company, and even managed to laugh several times throughout the very good film.

On the way home he relapsed into glumness, and was silent until just before the end of her street. Then he asked urgently, 'Can I talk to you, Finley? You might be able to give me the woman's angle on this.'

She couldn't find it in her heart to refuse him. She knew what was coming; he would tell her his side of his domestic drama and expect her to agree with him. If she didn't, he would counter-attack all her arguments and go away feeling gloomily that all women were alike, stupid and untrustworthy. But he was unhappy, and perhaps talking through his pain would ease it a little.

'Yes, all right, but I'll have to kick you out after a fairly short time. I'm bushed.'

He grunted an assent, no doubt already marshalling his arguments. It had begun to rain and the temperature, already low, had dropped considerably. Summer seemed an aeon away, lost with all the other summers of her life.

'Nasty east wind,' Tim remarked bitterly as they walked up the path together. 'I hate driving in the rain at night.'

Finley hid a slight smile. He was so absorbed in his unhappiness that it almost seemed that he was enjoying it.

Once inside she made him an omelette and a salad, made coffee and gave him aspirin for the headache he had developed. He ate and drank, and, cradling his coffee-cup in his hands, told her that Therese had left him because he didn't want children.

'Not just now,' he said. 'Of course, I want a family

eventually, but the timing's wrong.'

There were several reasons why the timing was wrong but, to Finley, it sounded as though Tim didn't want to give up his freedom to the gently dictatorial needs of a baby.

'How old is Therese?'

'Twenty-nine,' he told her fretfully. 'So she's getting on a bit. God, there are thousands of women who wait until the thirties.'

'How far into the thirties would you want her to wait?'

He didn't know. He muttered something about 'a few years' and finished his second cup of coffee, demanding to know why Therese should turn so bloody unreasonable when they'd agreed not to have children.

Finley was becoming a little exasperated at his self-centred attitude. He didn't seem to realise that Therese must have been very unhappy to have left him.

'Well, when is the time going to be right?' she asked.

Morosely he answered, 'Well, I want to go overseas——'

'Oh, Tim, I suppose no one ever did that with children?'

'You think I'm being unreasonable, don't you? Well, how's this for——'

'Look, I don't want to hear this. I just think by refusing even to discuss this thing, you've backed both of yourselves into a corner. Tell me, would you rather be unhappy with Therese and a baby than unhappy without her?'

He snorted at that, but acknowledged the hit. 'OK, OK,' he said wearily. 'I get the message, although why she wants to ruin a perfectly good set-up just to have kids, I'll never know.'

'Obviously the set-up isn't perfect for her.'

He laughed wryly, getting to his feet. 'I should have known better than to choose you for a confidante.

Relentlessly logical, that's you. Thanks for listening, I'm sorry if I bored your ears rigid.'

At the door he turned, astounding her by dropping a quick kiss on her cheek. 'You're a nice thing,' he said gruffly, 'even though I get the distinct feeling you might set the sisterhood on me. Goodnight.'

She pushed the door to quickly, her smile fading as she stood for a moment with closed eyes. Everyone seemed to be suffering. Poor Therese. And poor Tim, who probably would never understand.

On the wall was a framed poster advertising an exhibition of icons. The dark green mount set the gold of the painting into glowing, rapturous prominence, in which the dark, solemn faces of the mother and child became the focal point.

'Oh, lord,' she said wearily, then jumped as behind her the doorbell pealed an imperative summons.

Tim must have forgotten something.

But the man was Blake, almost filling the aperture as he came through the door, rain gleaming on his darkened hair and his eyes as cold and remote as slivers of golden quartz.

CHAPTER TEN

SHE might have gasped his name, she didn't really know what she said, but his stance and the expression on his face made her go cold with fright.

'What's happened? she gasped, tugging at the hand which had fastened around her wrist. 'Blake, what is it?'

'I find that I don't enjoy sitting outside your flat for almost an hour, wondering whether you are actually in bed with the man I saw you come with,' he said icily. 'I don't enjoy it at all.'

Finley froze. A quick look revealed implacable features; she lifted her chin and said between her teeth, 'You had only to knock on the door and I'd have let you in. You didn't have to skulk outside like some sleazy private detective.'

His grip on her wrist tightened. He said nothing as he began to tow her into the bedroom.

'I prefer,' he said deliberately, 'to find these things out myself.'

Anger made her bold. 'How? By checking the bed?'

'No. By checking you.'

Disappointment fuelled her anger as she realised what he meant. She tried to jerk free but for the first time he made her appreciate how puny her strength was against his. He did not hurt, but he dealt with her struggles coolly and impersonally.

'No!' she spat as he removed her clothes. 'No, I don't want you.'

'A pity, because I happen to want you.'

He tossed her on to the bed and crushed her into the mattress with his big body.

Her small teeth sought his throat; she bit and he

drove home, thrusting into a body that incredibly, treacherously, was ready for him.

What followed could never have been called making love. All that was primitive in them was brought to the surface in a ferocious yet compelling satisfying surge of power, until at last Finley convulsed, calling his name through swollen lips, and his body shuddered with answering tremors.

A long time later she said, 'I didn't go to bed with him.'

'Oh, God, I know that,' he said, self-contempt abrasive through his voice. 'My love, my love, what have I done to you?'

He held her gently, touching her lips with his, stroking her small body with a hand which shook.

'It doesn't matter,' she whispered, breathing in the dear scent of him.

They lay entwined until he said, 'It matters. I can't even say that I believed that you were making love. I waited for an hour for you to come home, and then it was with him. I sat out there like some wronged husband and worked myself up into a stupid jealous rage until I was murderous with it. I didn't dare come in until he had gone. Finley, I've never needed anyone before. I wasn't going to see you until I came over for a meeting in a fortnight's time, but I couldn't stay away that long.'

'You resent me,' she said sadly.

He looked haunted, almost gaunt, and she pulled his head down and cradled it against her breasts.

'I don't want to feel like this,' he said tensely. 'I feel as though the personality I've always taken for granted is being bled away by my need for you. I've never hurt a woman in my life, and look at you ...'

His appalled gaze took in her swollen mouth, the marks he had put on her pale skin. Anguished, he whispered, 'I'm sorry. I love you, yet I've done this to you. It mustn't happen again.'

She went very still, like an animal hoping against hope to avoid attack. 'What do you mean?' Her voice, she noted vaguely, was steady.

'If I can't trust myself I mustn't see you again.' He lowered his mouth to each of the bruises, and she melted in mindless appreciation.

'It doesn't matter,' she said again, gone beyond hope now.

He said nothing, cuddling her close in an embrace which held love and shame and complete and utter finality. Tenderly, her fingers threaded through his hair, dry now and warm against the fine moulding of his skull. Without words, withour tears, they said goodbye.

The tears came when he left, tears which soaked her pillow and left her with stinging eyes and a headache severe enough to warrant a pain-killer.

Looking back, she could never remember the days and weeks which followed with any degree of clarity. She was only able to survive by cutting free of the woman who loved Blake Caird. At the hospital she functioned well, giving everything to her work. Because it was dangerous not to, she ate well and slept at least eight hours every night. She was rather surprised at her ability to do this. She expected the hours away from work to be long and difficult, but she filled them with study, and went for long walks with the dog, and forced herself to socialise so that there were few times when she was alone with her despair.

Nobody realised that she was slowly bleeding to death inside. Except perhaps Sue, who watched her closely but said nothing. Possibly the pediatric registrar, that shrewd formidable woman, had some suspicion, but although occasionally Finley felt the other woman's gaze rest thoughtfully on her, she too said nothing.

In a way it was quite easy to seal off the portion of herself that hurt. Mostly it worked. She learned to dread the times when it didn't and she was overwhelmed with hunger for him, the sight and scent and feel of him, the keen joys of companionship, the deep pleasure of a communion which was more than mental and physical.

Then she would find herself weeping and in the desolation she would hear Blackie's sympathetic whine. She would stroke his shaggy poll and sob with the defeated weariness of one who has endured too much. Afterwards, she would have to use cover-stick to hide the shadows under her eyes.

Slowly, she began to realise that she would never again feel for any man what she had felt for Blake. He was her first love, perhaps her only romantic love. If she married she might find happiness, but it would not be the ecstasy he promised. Although in time her memories of Blake would lose their keen aching edge, never again would she know that rapturous certainty.

Autumn was edging grumpily into winter when Tim said one day, very casually, 'Oh, by the way, Therese is pregnant.'

'Is she now? How do you feel about it?'

He had told her a month before, even more casually, that they were once more living together but, because he had not mentioned it again, neither had she.

Now he looked resigned. 'Well, all right, I suppose. We went to a marriage guidance counsellor. It was a bit weird, she made it obvious that she wasn't going to take sides or act as a referee, so after a few false starts we actually had to sit down and communicate.'

'Not easy?'

'No,' he said gruffly. 'Well, hell, you think you know all there is to know about your lover, and then they hit you with a whole chunk of personality you've never come across before.'

Join the club, she thought wearily, recalling Blake's words that last night together. She hid her emotions with a smile, and was answered by Tim's slightly shamefaced one.

'Well, that's how it seemed! She'd been reading stupid magazine articles and she was afraid she might not conceive once she got past thirty. Hell, she only had to ask! I'm a doctor!'

'Perhaps she felt you might not be entirely impartial.'

'She might have been right at that,' he conceded a little reluctantly. 'Anyway, I had no idea she was fretting over it like that.'

'How happy are you really over this pregnancy?'

He looked shifty. 'Actually, I'm not ecstatic, but I always wanted children, it was just selfishness that made me kick up a fuss. Once I realised that . . . well, it was pretty low behaviour. Everyone has to compromise, don't they?'

His words stuck in Finley's mind. Their patent truth nagged at her mind until she wondered whether there was any sort of compromise possible in her situation. She would, she thought, be only too willing, but Blake . . . Right from the start he had made it clear that Motuaroha was the one constant in his life. The island was not negotiable. And neither was her profession.

Normally she did not go into the heart of Auckland, and especially not in the rain, but one viciously wet Saturday morning she woke in such depression that almost without making any decision she drove into town. There were several things she needed to do; she had her hair trimmed back to her normal smooth cut, then went into her favourite bookshop and bought herself a copy of a novel she had been promising herself before drifting across to the paperback section.

'Weather like this positively demands something large and glossy and escapist, doesn't it?' The voice was deep, its normal coolness warmed by a conspiritorial note.

Finley swung about to meet the eyes the colour of lapis lazuli. Clary Caird!

'Hello,' she said awkwardly. 'Yes, it does. I thought a nice fat historical.'

'With pirates?'

'Oh, definitely pirates,' Finley agreed, nodding. 'Lots of swashbuckling.'

They smiled at each other, this time without awkwardness.

'I can recommend this one.' Clary indicated a substantial tome, on the cover of which a red-headed woman wielded a large sword beside a pirate of unnaturally handsome features. 'The lurid cover belies the book. It's well written and the story doesn't slacken from the first page to the last. Also, the characters have reasons for their actions.'

'You've sold it.'

They took their purchases to the till, Clary answering Finley's query with a short, lively description of the mayhem her son had managed to create that morning, before finishing in doting tones, 'But I shouldn't complain. The Cairds seem to have cornered the market in determination.'

Haven't they just, Finley thought numbly. Aloud, she made a noise which could have signified agreement, then got through the small transaction at the counter with a smile which felt pinned on. She could hardly wait for the moment when they said goodbye.

But as they walked out of the shop Clary said, 'Why don't we have lunch together? I'll give Morgan a ring. He adores baby-sitting John and won't mind in the least if I stay out to a meal. There's a rather nice restaurant in High Street . . .'

She looked so enthusiastic that Finley couldn't refuse. Besides, what was there to go home to? A flat empty except for Blackie, and he was quite happy on Sue's floor playing with Pippa.

So she agreed, and five minutes later was being tenderly tucked into a chair by a waiter whose solicitude was almost overpowering. 'They know you here,' she observed.

Clary grinned. 'They do. They always manage to make me feel as though I'm a lovable but dim-witted younger sister. I think it's probably because the first time we came here I was pregnant, and I fainted. They were horrified, but so kind. Now they view me with some foreboding but, after reassuring themselves that I'm not in a delicate condition, they relax.'

Surprisingly, Finley ate well, enjoying her companion's conversation until the coffee arrived. Clary smiled her thanks at the waiter, leaned forward and said, 'Now, this is the part we've both been bracing ourselves for. Why are you and Blake trying to drive each other into an early grave?'

Finley froze. All the misery of the past months gathered in her throat, clogging it. She could only shake her head and avoid that altogether too astute gaze from the other side of the table.

But Clary, having found the courage to bring up the subject, was ruthless. 'He was at our place last week. He arrived out of the blue, looking like—well, haggard is a kind way to describe him. After we'd fed him I retired and left them to it.' She smiled faintly. 'He and Morgan are very close, you know, more like best friends than cousins. He just about drank Morgan's whisky dry. And that is *not* like Blake. Morgan is worried about him. He said he didn't get drunk, just savage. He is bitterly unhappy, Finley, and so are you. You look as though the sky has fallen in on your world. Can't you find some sort of solution?'

Finley drank her coffee, swallowing hard to clear the obstruction in her throat. In a hard, husky voice she said, 'Do you think we haven't tried?'

'I think you are both too close to the situation to think clearly. Is there no way you could come to a compromise?'

That damned word again! Starkly Finley asked, 'How?'

'Well, if, for example, you went into general practice.'
'On Motuaroha?'
'No, you wouldn't be able to live there, of course.'
Finley considered this, her narrow brows drawn together. 'Yes. Yes, I could do that. It would be a wrench—but oh, it's impossible! Motuaroha is the great love of Blake's life.'
'I think he's discovering that that isn't really so,' Clary said wisely.

She left the subject then and they went their separate ways. After a few days, Finley managed to push the memory of their meeting to the back of their minds. But the hope that Clary had roused was not so easily dismissed. As winter tightened its grip on the weather Finley waited, until gradually, painfully, all hope fled. Motuaroha had won.

She forced herself to continue the social life she had embarked upon, glad that it was within circumscribed medical circles. There were few chances of meeting anyone from the agricultural world.

After a party at Tim's, with a radiant Therese very much in evidence, she slept late and deeply until the persistent angry peal of the doorbell woke her. She was so disorientated that she opened it without even putting up the chain.

To the man who stood grimly waiting in the rain she looked exhausted, dark circles under eyes revealing how hard she had been driving herself.

She gaped and he said impatiently, 'Let me in, Finley, it's damned cold out here.'

Memories of the last time she had seen him, of his fierce, barbaric behaviour, flooded through her brain, jerking her from her lethargy. She made to slam the door. His eyes gleamed with angry insolence as he pushed inside, slamming the door behind him. A hard smile pulled at his mouth and he stood silently daring her to object.

'Come in,' she said tonelessly, because her body was shaking in a tide of drenching sweetness. She knew what was going to happen, and she knew she wouldn't fight him. Not ever again. She was trapped within the boundaries of his heart and there was nothing she could do about it.

Squaring her shoulders, she walked past him into the sitting-room, looking around it with distaste. It was quite obvious that nothing had been done to it for days; a thin film of dust lay over everything. The flowers were dead and it was cold and dank.

'Do you want a cup of coffee?'

He shook his head. 'You look like death. Go and have a bath or a shower, whatever will revive you most, and get dressed.'

She hid her disappointment with words. 'Dictatorial swine,' she said without heat.

The broad shoulders shrugged. 'That's the way I am.' His eyes glinted as they swept over her defiant little figure. Softly and pleasantly he added, 'And I can make you do anything I want, so off you go, my heart, before I strip you myself.'

In that mood he was dangerous. Finley bit her lip but she obeyed, taking out her anger at being ordered around by prolonging the shower for as long as she could stand it. She pulled on tweed slacks and waistcoat over a pale apricot lambswool jersey and blowdried her hair, wondering at the occasional sound she heard from the sitting-room.

Her nostrils were tantalised by the smell of coffee as soon as she opened the door. He had built a fire in the fireplace, and the leaping flames warmed the now dusted room. He had, she thought warily, the capacity to constantly surprise her with some new facet of his personality.

'Sit down at the table,' he commanded from the kitchen.

He poached her an egg, insisted she eat a slice of toast and drank coffee with her. When he wasn't looking, she watched him with avid eyes.

He had lost the gauntness of his last visit but the harsh features were tightened by strain, and there were deeper lines by his mouth. She felt her heart go out to him, and forgot to hide her survey so that, inevitably, he caught her staring.

'Been tough, has it?'

She nodded, giving up any pretence.

He smiled sardonically. 'We put ourselves through hell. Well, are you ready to go?'

Confused, she asked, 'Go? Go where?'

'You'll see. We'll leave Blackie with your neighbours this——'

'Blake, how did you know I was free today?'

'Same way as I know Blackie is at the neighbour's.' He got up and pulled her from her chair. 'I rang her up, swore her to secrecy, and asked her. You'll need a coat and umbrella. Have you any gumboots? Good, bring them too, you'll need them. Make sure you're wearing enough to keep you warm.'

He refused to answer any questions, remaining infuriatingly silent until she lost patience and refused to go with him. Then he grinned, picked her up and carried her out to his car, ignoring completely her angry protests. Fuming, she sat silently as he took the big vehicle through the quiet streets until they reached the motorway, and he headed north.

Then he said, 'Humour me, my heart.'

And she relented, reading in the words the past months of loneliness and despair. They talked of the island, of the people Finley had come to know, then as the powerful car ate up the miles, they relapsed into silence. Finley was content to be beside him, watching the rain stream down the windows, secure in his dear presence.

The rain stopped at the base of the Brynderwyn Hills just as they left the main road for a narrow gravel road which headed inland across the Waipu flats and through another, lower range of hills. The countryside was fresh and green, pockets of native bush in the gullies, small streams racing in red-brown confusion between their banks, scrub and rushes and tired fences. Clearly, the land had not been given the care that was evident on Motuaroha's acres.

At last they climbed a hill and came over it to see a much wider valley. Blake's lean hands were competent and quick, even when a huge milk tanker hurtled around a corner at them, slightly too fast for comfort. He swore beneath his breath, but both drivers were skilled and they sorted themselves out without too much trouble.

Just after that Blake turned the car onto a narrow, rutted drive along the hillside, finally pulling to a halt outside a house which was clearly derelict. Finley stared at him. His hands clenched on to the wheel, then relaxed. With an effort he said, 'Right, let's have a look.'

The whole place was derelict. The woolshed was huge but rickety, and had clearly not been used for years. The implement sheds were slowly sinking into the long grass. The house looked like a favourite residence of bats.

'It's been used as a run-off,' he said in answer to a question, 'which is why the buildings are ruins. This place as well as the block next door belonged to an old chap who died recently. His family are only too keen to sell.'

'It doesn't look as though he cared much for it.'

'He lost heart, I think.' He spoke absently, kicked a fence-post which promptly collapsed, and dusted slightly grubby hands together. 'It has an immense amount of potential. There's a good mixture of soils, some suitable for kiwi-fruit and other horticultural lines, and it's well-watered.'

Finley nodded, convinced now that he had brought her

there for a specific reason and afraid to ask what it was
About a mile across the undulating valley floor a cluste
of houses indicated a village; she picked out a church
spire and a football field, a larger expanse of roof which
probably indicated a hall, and the neat government-issue
buildings of a school.

'Although this is the logical site for the homestead this
one is too far gone to renovate. My redoubtable aunt took
one look at it and advised bulldozing it down.'

'It certainly doesn't look salvageable,' Finley agreed
Her voice firmed; plucking up courage she asked, 'Have
you bought the place, Blake?'

'I have an option on it.' He removed her hand from the
pocket of her jacket and tucked it into the crook of his
arm, setting with long strides back to the car. As they
reached it he said, 'The decision rests with you.'

She opened her mouth but had no time to speak before
he bundled her into the warmth of the car. Finley took off
her gumboots and put them in the back, turning to say
that it was impossible, that she couldn't . . .

Forestalling her, he said in a voice as unrevealing as
his expression. 'They need a doctor here. The present one
is over retiring age. He doesn't want to give up entirely
he's prepared to do nights and the weekends after he's
retired. Apparently there's not much to do then anyway
The nearest hospital, a cottage hospital, is about twenty
kilometres away. It deals mainly with maternity cases
The valley has been dreaming away for the last thirty
years, but it's about to move. Already two farmers have
set up horticultural blocks. In five years' time the valley
will probably be cut up into orchards. It won't be long
before there will be a big enough practice for two full
time doctors.'

'But Motuaroha,' she protested, unable to take in what
he was suggesting.

'I can leave Motuaroha,' he said evenly. His half
closed eyes were fixed on her face, flat and unwinking. '

don't deny it will be hard, but a man who is tied to one place is dependent on that place. I'm as adaptable as, I hope, you are.'

She sat with head bent. Beneath the dead trees in the orchard bloomed clumps of paper-white jonquils. She had picked a handful and wrapped the stems in a tissue. Their sweet scent filled the car as she admired the tiny cream cups and white, star-shaped petals behind.

She looked up, but not at him, at the valley below. If he came to live here she would always wonder how life as a paediatrician might have been, but she would never regret giving it up.

Slowly, her head turned, and she met the impassive scrutiny of the man beside her. All of the gold had seeped from his eyes; they were hard, dull brown, without warmth. She could not bear him to look like that.

'Yes,' she said.

For a long moment he said nothing. Then he said quietly, 'Thank God,' and the hands which had been so rigidly locked on to the wheel relaxed, and she was hauled against him while he fumbled for the catch which lowered the back of his seat.

'I love you,' he whispered, his cheek cold on hers.

Finley had dropped the jonquils. Their pervasive perfume mingled with his own special scent as she lifted a hand to his face, traced the high cheekbone, and came to an abrupt halt at the vulnerable curve of his closed eyes.

'Blake?' she whispered shakily.

'I love you so much. My heart, it's been hell. I thought I'd never see you again. And I realised that what I felt for you was greater than anything else. I would give up anything, everything for you, but I didn't know whether you loved me enough to give up your dreams.'

'Oh, I think I was coming to accept that my dreams weren't much without you,' she said wryly, too suddenly whisked from despair to joy to be able to appreciate the

difference yet. She lay curled in his lap, noting with som
surprise that the windows had fogged over.

His mouth searched through the hair over her templ
to come to rest against her forehead. She felt the eve
present awareness, knew that he was tense with longing
yet somehow it did not matter now, there was no urgency
none of the barely hidden desperation which ha
characterised their loving up until then.

'If you have a birth certificate we can apply for
marriage licence tomorrow and get married three day
later. We'll have to have a long-distance marriage unti
you can organise yourself out of the hospital, but I wan
you married to me.' He spoke urgently, his voic
persuasive and coaxing.

'OK,' she replied.

He was silent, then he laughed silently, his arm
tightening about her. 'When you surrender you go th
whole hog, don't you? Don't you mind the thought o
such a hurried marriage?'

'No, if you don't mind a bride who has to go to worl
the morning after the wedding.'

'I'll resent it like hell, but only because I won't wan
you out of my bed for weeks. What about clothes?'

'What about clothes? What clothes?'

'Don't you want to splash out on a wedding dress?'

She laughed and reached up to kiss him. Hours later, i
seemed, she said dreamily, 'Keep that up and I doubt i
you'll be able to prise me out of your bed with a crowba
I have a wedding dress. I bought it in a bout of shee
masochism a month ago. I told myself I'd wear it t
parties, but I knew it was my wedding dress.' Her voic
trembled. 'I just didn't think I'd ever get to wear it.'

'My dearest girl, my precious heart, don't.' He tilte
her head so that he could touch his tongue to the tears sh
could not hide. The erotic little caress made her shudde
but effectively stopped her weeping. She sighed an
turned her head into his throat.

'What happens to Motuaroha? Are you going to sell it?' she asked. She waited tensely for his answer.

'No, it will always be there. I'll have to go across from time to time, just as I do for the other businesses. We'll have holidays there, and perhaps one of our children will want to live there. I have an excellent manager lined up for it. Incidentally, Phil would rather like to come here if you'd like her to. We'll need a housekeeper and her son is approaching high-school age. She and her husband don't want him to leave home so this would be ideal for them.'

'Ideal for us, too,' she said, sliding her hand beneath the hem of his shirt, her fingers revelling in the warm strong body which was now hers. She smiled secretly as she heard his soft groan and felt his heart beat pick up speed. 'I love you,' she said.

'Shall we go home and you can show me how much?'

Her breath caught in her throat. 'Yes,' she said, and leaned up and whispered in his ear exactly how she would show him.

His eyes gleamed beneath his lowered lashes. He put her into her seat and said lazily, 'I suppose that's your medical knowledge coming to the fore. Are you sure it's possible?'

'We'll find out, shall we?'

'We will,' he promised, winding down the window to let air in to clear their vision. He looked across at her, wickedly, totally confident, and smiling with such happiness and relief that she was dazzled. 'Just think of all the things we still have to find out about each other,' he said as he set the big car in motion. 'And all the time in the world to do it.'

It had begun to rain again, a miserable spitting drizzle which made driving difficult but inside the car was warmth and love and joy. It would always be summer, Finley decided rapturously, in this country which was now their home, this country of the heart.

Harlequin Presents

Coming Next Month

1047　RECKLESS　Amanda Carpenter
A routine assignment to South America turns into a nightmare when Leslie's flight is hijacked. She draws on all her strength to save fellow journalist Scott Bennett, only to discover the real test is of her ability to love again.

1048　STRIKE AT THE HEART　Emma Darcy
Sunny King is everything Jackie Mulholland disapproves of: rich, reckless and overwhelmingly arrogant. So she's disturbed by the attraction he seems to hold for her two young sons. She's even more disturbed by her own attraction to him.

1049　CARLISLE PRIDE　Leigh Michaels
Brooke has more than her share of pride. It was pride that made her break her engagement to Ty Marshall after finding him in her stepmother's arms; and it's pride that now makes her refuse to sell Oakley Manor…but refusing Ty again will cost more than pride.

1050　TAGGART'S WOMAN　Carole Mortimer
To inherit her rightful share of the family airline business, Heather is forced to marry her late father's partner, Daniel Taggart. For Heather the arrangement seems a little like hell—and heaven.

1051　TRUE ENCHANTER　Susan Napier
Joanna's not impressed by the superficial glamour of the film world, which is why she's the perfect chaperone for her actress niece. But she's not what director Richard Marlow expects. She can see right through him, as he does her. Have they both met their match?

1052　OPEN TO INFLUENCE　Frances Roding
A girl on her own, hopelessly in love with her married boss and without a job because of it, is hardly the ideal guardian for an orphaned three year old. So Rosemary is in no position to refuse Nicholas Powers, even if it means giving up a life—and love—of her own.

1053　BROKEN SILENCE　Kate Walker
When Jill negotiates her wages as a temporary nanny to Luke Garrett's small son, she doesn't bargain for the claim her employer makes on her own heart. She should have.

1054　THIS MAN'S MAGIC　Stephanie Wyatt
By asking her father for an introduction to Lucas Armory, Sorrel starts a chain of events that turns her life upside down. For Luke doesn't believe she's Felix Valentine's daughter, and worse, he accuses her of stealing his company's latest jewelry designs.

Available in January wherever paperback books are sold, or through Harlequin Reader Service:

In the U.S.
901 Fuhrmann Blvd.
P.O. Box 1397
Buffalo, N.Y. 14240-1397

In Canada
P.O. Box 603
Fort Erie, Ontario
L2A 5X3

An enticing
new historical romance!

Spring Will Come

SHERRY DeBorde

It was 1852, and the steamy South was in its last hours of gentility. Camille Braxton Beaufort went searching for the one man she knew she could trust, and under his protection had her first lesson in love....

Available in October at your favorite retail outlet, or reserve your copy for September shipping by sending your name, address, zip or postal code, along with a check or money order for $4.70 (includes 75¢ postage and handling) payable to Worldwide Library to:

In the U.S.

Worldwide Library
901 Fuhrmann Blvd.
P.O. Box 1325
Buffalo, NY 14269-1325

In Canada

Worldwide Library
P.O. Box 609
Fort Erie, Ontario
L2A 5X3

Please specify book title with your order.

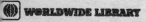 WORLDWIDE LIBRARY

SPR-1

ATTRACTIVE, SPACE SAVING BOOK RACK

Display your most prized novels on this handsome and sturdy book rack. The hand-rubbed walnut finish will blend into your library decor with quiet elegance, providing a practical organizer for your favorite hard-or soft-covered books.

Only $9.95

Approximately 16" x 8" when assembled

Assembles in seconds

To order, rush your name, address and zip code, along with a check or money order for $10.70* ($9.95 plus 75¢ postage and handling) payable to *Harlequin Reader Service*:

Harlequin Reader Service
Book Rack Offer
901 Fuhrmann Blvd.
P.O. Box 1396
Buffalo, NY 14269-1396

Offer not available in Canada.

*New York and Iowa residents add appropriate sales tax.

*Harlequin
Intrigue*

In October
Watch for the new look of

Harlequin Intrigue
...because romance can be quite an
adventure!

Each time, Harlequin Intrigue brings you
great stories, mixing a contemporary,
sophisticated romance with the surprising
twists and turns of a puzzler...romance with
"something more."

Plus...
in next month's publications of Harlequin
Intrigue we offer you the chance to win one of
four mysterious and exciting weekends. Don't
miss the opportunity! Read the October
Harlequin Intrigues!

J-INT-R

Coming Soon
from Harlequin...

GIFTS FROM THE HEART

**Watch for it
in February**

HEART-1
February 88

Deep in the heart of Africa lay mankind's most awesome secret. Could they find Eden . . . and the grave of Eve?

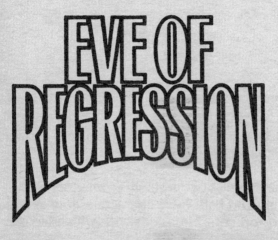

JOHN ARTHUR LONG

A spellbinding novel that combines a fascinating premise with all the ingredients of an edge-of-the-seat read: passion, adventure, suspense and danger.

Available in January at your favorite retail outlet, or reserve your copy for December shipping by sending your name, address, zip or postal code along with a check or money order for $4.70 (includes 75¢ for postage and handling) payable to Worldwide Library to:

In the U.S.	In Canada
Worldwide Library	Worldwide Library
901 Fuhrmann Blvd.	P.O. Box 609
Box 1325	Fort Erie, Ontario
Buffalo, NY 14269-1325	L2A 5X3

Please specify book title with your order.   EVE-1

🌐® **WORLDWIDE LIBRARY** ®

If *YOU* enjoyed this book,
your daughter may enjoy

Keepsake

Romances from

CROSSWINDS

Keepsake is a series of tender, funny, down-to-
earth romances for younger teens.

The simple boy-meets-girl romances have
lively and believable characters, lots of action
and romantic situations with which teens can
identify.

Available now wherever books are sold.

ADULT